Newfangled Fairy Tales

Book #2

Edited by Bruce Lansky

Meadowbrook Press
Distributed by Simon & Schuster
New York

ISSN: 1093-5339

Publisher's ISBN: 0-88166-317-4
Simon & Schuster Ordering # 0-689-82211-1

Editor: Bruce Lansky
Coordinating Editor: Jason Sanford
Copyeditor: Christine Zuchora-Walske
Production Manager: Joe Gagne
Production Assistant: Danielle White
Cover Illustrator: Joy Allen

© 1998 by Meadowbrook Creations

All stories are copyrighted and published with the permission of the authors.

pp. 1 "Rumpelstiltskin, Private Eye" © 1998 by Jason Sanford; pp. 15 "The Girl Who Wanted to Be a Princess" © 1998 by Bruce Lansky; pp. 29 and 91 "The Little Tailor" and "Hansel and Gretel" © 1998 by Timothy Tocher; pp. 41 "A Thoroughly Modern Rapunzel" © 1998 by Jude Mandell; pp. 51 "The Fairy Godfather" © 1998 by Liya Lev Oertel; pp. 63 "The Clever Princess Who Slept on a Pea" © 1998 by Debra Tracy; pp. 71 "The Gold Ring" © 1998 by Rita Schlachter; pp. 81 "Red Riding Hood and the Scrawny Little Wolf" © 1998 by Mary Quattlebaum; pp. 101 "Katie and the Dragon" © 1998 by Risa Hutson.

Published by Meadowbrook Press, 5451 Smetana Drive; Minnetonka, Minnesota 55343

BOOK TRADE DISTRIBUTION by Simon & Schuster, a division of Simon and Schuster, Inc., 1230 Avenue of the Americas, New York, NY 10020

02 01 00 99 98   12 11 10 9 8 7 6 5 4 3 2 1

Printed in the United States of America

Contents

Acknowledgments

Thank you to all the young men and women
who served on a reading panel for this project:

Corey Bertelsen, Katherine Bryan, Steve Burton, Kelsey
Carlson, Alec Chambers, Morgan Dewanz, Randi Edquist,
Rikki Egge, Kara Erstad, Sara Ford, Nolan Fredrickson,
Alyssa Hamre, Patrick Hayes, Alisia Irvin, Katelyn Isom,
Daniel Jasper, Alynn Kakuk, Marin Krause, Katie Kroeck,
Marisa Lafontaine, Thomas Langle, Gina Leone, Taylor R.
Mallon, Bryan Mattson, Glenn D. Melcher, Charles Miller,
Ali Moeller, Andrew Myers, Stacie Noha, Whitney Owens,
Kristin Peterson, Lisa Peterson, Morgan Pittman, Marissa
Rattray, Talles Ross, Jon Routh, Elisabeth Smeltzer, Stacie
Sturtevant, Brianne Theisen, Andrea Thompson, Matthew
Tody, Joey Young, Ben Zweber

Introduction

Nothing has to stay the same forever—especially if it doesn't make sense. Take fairy tales, for example. I think you'll agree with me that a princess shouldn't have to marry a knight she doesn't love (even if the knight does defeat a dragon), that no one can weave straw into gold, that no prince in his right mind would marry a princess who complains about a pea under twenty mattresses, and that the brave little tailor was actually a vain braggart. If you agree that these things don't make sense, then you'll love this collection of fairy tales.

We've taken some of the most famous fairy-tale characters and twisted things around to make their stories a lot more fun to read. Rumple-what's-his-name is now a private investigator who uncovers the straw-into-gold scam. And, speaking of scams, a clever princess named Katie makes a deal with a dragon so she won't have to marry a pompous knight. There's also a story about a fairy godfather who disagrees with most of the advice that fairy godmothers are supposed to give, and a story about Little Red Riding Hood, who gets angry at the wolf for refusing to eat her sick grandmother.

I suppose my favorite story—perhaps because I wrote it— is about Michelle Koszlowski, the daughter of a plumber from Sheboygan, Michigan. She loves to buy clothes and hates to work, and constantly wishes she were a princess. Well, as the saying goes, be careful what you wish for, because it might come true.

I think by now you've figured out that these are not your

run-of-the-mill Grimm fairy tales. They're different—and you will be too after you read them, because the underlying message of these stories is that things don't have to be the way they always were. Particularly if they don't make sense.

Happy reading!

Bruce Lansky

Bruce Lansky

Rumpelstiltskin, Private Eye

BY JASON SANFORD

The name on my door says it all: "Rumpelstiltskin, Private Eye." I'm the one people turn to when they're in a jam. Remember that crazy wolf who blew down those pigs' houses? I caught him. When Jack stole the giant's golden-egg-laying hen, I tracked him down.

'Course, things don't always go so smoothly. Take my last case. What started out as a good mystery almost ended with me in the dungeon . . . all because of the captain of the guard, a miller's daughter, and a whole lot of straw.

It began on a rainy Friday afternoon. I was watching an old Sherlock Holmes movie on TV when the miller walked in the door. I recognized him right away; he and his daughter had been in the news a lot lately. Rumor had it she'd been spinning straw into gold for the king, but I didn't believe that for a minute.

"I'm looking for a private eye," the miller said.

"That's me. Have a seat."

I poured the miller a glass of soda pop. He was a scraggly looking man, clothes patched and double patched. He needed a haircut worse than Rapunzel.

The miller sipped his drink, then sighed. "It's my daughter," he said. "She's been kidnapped by the king."

I whistled. The king was a little greedy—he said he'd marry anyone who could increase his stash of golden cash. Still, he was a nice guy and I had trouble believing that he would kidnap anyone. "Can your daughter really spin straw into gold?"

The miller shook his head. "Of course not. What fairy tale do you think this is?"

"Then why would the king kidnap her?"

"Well . . ." the miller said, looking a little sheepish. "I was bowling with the captain of the palace guard, and I happened to mention how intelligent my daughter is, how beautiful she is, how . . ." he paused. "How she can spin straw into gold. Next day she was gone."

I groaned. There's no telling how many kids have gotten into trouble because their parents brag a little too much.

"I guess the captain told the king what I said," the miller concluded. "Can you get my daughter out of the castle?"

I thought about it. I'd had a run-in with the captain of the guard before—caught him taking a bribe from Puss in Boots. It didn't surprise me that he was mixed up in this. But why would the king keep the miller's daughter in the castle if she couldn't spin straw into gold? Surely he'd have discovered that little fact by now.

I told the miller I'd take the case. I loved a good mystery, and this one was a puzzler. I shook hands with the miller, then ran to the castle. It was still raining, but I figured, hey, this'll save me the trouble of bathing tonight.

I stopped at the guard house by the drawbridge. My friend Happy was on duty. He and I had been the first really short people to make it through the Guard Academy. After I quit to become a private eye, Happy'd stayed on and became a lieutenant. He said being a castle guard paid better than working for Snow White, and it was easier than being self-employed like me.

"What's up, Rump?" Happy asked.

"I need to see the king," I said. "Got a case that involves him."

Happy shook his head. "No can do, bud. The captain of the guard said no visitors today, and I'm doing just what he says. The captain's got a major case of hay fever and he's in a nasty mood."

"Now why would hay fever be bothering him inside the castle?"

Happy grinned. "The captain found someone to spin straw into gold for the king. His Highness was so excited he ordered us to collect every bit of straw in the kingdom. One of the three pigs came by today and yelled at me because we even took down his straw house."

"Can the miller's daughter really spin straw into gold?" I asked.

Happy nodded. "Seen it myself—straw goes in the main storeroom at night; gold comes out the next day. The king's making a bundle."

I was just about to ask Happy to let me in the castle to snoop around when the captain of the guard appeared.

"What is *he* doing here?" the captain barked at Happy.

"I'm looking for the miller's daughter," I said. "Seen her?"

The captain glared at me. As he leaned close to me, I caught a whiff of him. Phew! His uniform was filthy, and he smelled like rotten fish. "I don't talk to little creeps like you, Bumplestiltskin," he said.

"Rumpelstiltskin," I said. "The name's Rumpelstiltskin." The captain had never been able to remember my name.

"Whatever," the captain said. "Happy, follow your orders. No visitors." He walked back into the castle.

Happy sighed. He didn't like the captain, either.

"Where's the miller's daughter?" I asked.

"She's in the storeroom," Happy whispered, "but you'd better stay away. You get anywhere near her and the captain'll be after you like the Big Bad Wolf."

I thanked Happy and walked away. Things just didn't make sense. No one could spin straw into gold, but it sure sounded as if that were happening. I had to get in the castle to see for myself—but how? The castle walls were forty feet tall, and the rain made them as slick as ice. I looked down at the moat and saw water shooting out of a drainpipe.

Bingo, I thought. Every room in the castle had a

large drain on the floor to let water out.

Later that night, after the rain had stopped, I swam across the moat and squirmed like a worm through the drainpipe. Talk about disgusting—mushy garbage and rats were everywhere. I even got a bath in some old fish stew that someone had dumped down the drain.

Soon the drainpipe widened into a sewer. It was so dark in there, I had to feel my way along the sewer wall. Suddenly I stumbled over some heavy bags of trash. One of the bags slumped onto me as I went sprawling in the muck. I wiggled out from under it and kept groping along. Eventually I found the pipe leading to the storeroom. As I eased up the room's drain cover, it clanked softly on the stone floor.

"Who's there?" a voice snapped.

I looked around and saw a young woman sitting by a spinning wheel in one corner of the room.

"My name's Rumpelstiltskin," I said. "I'm a private eye. Your father sent me to help you."

"Great," she said. "I thought I'd be stuck here until not-so-happily ever after." Suddenly she wrinkled her nose. "Phew!" she said, waving her hand at me.

"Yeah, well," I said. "Real-life rescues tend to be messier than in fairy tales."

I crawled out of the drain and stood up. "The cleanest escape would be out the window," I said as I approached her. Then it hit me: the miller's daughter had supposedly been spinning straw into gold all night, but there was no gold—and only a little straw—in the room.

"Aren't we missing something here?" I asked. "Where's all the straw and gold?"

"Oh, the captain's already stashed the straw. As for the gold . . . well, I suppose you'll be taking the blame for that."

Blame for what? I thought. Suddenly an alarm went off in my head. I'd been set up! I tried to run, but the woman grabbed me. She was a full two feet taller than me and held me in a half nelson.

"I've got the thief!" she yelled, tightening her grip on my neck. "Guards! Guards!"

"No," I choked. "I'm here to help you."

"I don't need your help," she said. "I'm going to be a queen."

I couldn't believe my ears. Before I could say anything, the storeroom door opened, and in walked the captain and a couple of guards.

"Looks like we've caught the thief," the captain said.

"I'm not a thief."

The captain chuckled.

"You made it easy, Bumpletallskin," he said.

"Rumpelstiltskin," I said. "The name's Rumpelstiltskin."

"Whatever," the captain said. He pulled out a handkerchief and sneezed. "Anyway, I knew you couldn't ignore a good mystery."

"What's going on?" I asked. "Tricking the king into believing the miller's daughter can spin straw into gold isn't going to do anything for you."

The captain laughed. "We'll see," he said. "Arrest him."

Gee, I thought, the Wicked Witch hasn't got anything on this guy. Still, you don't get to be a P.I. if you can't improvise. I pushed my shoe under some straw and kicked it up into the captain's face. He exploded into a fit of coughs and sneezes as the other guards tried to help him.

"Gotta love hay fever," I said to the miller's daughter as I stomped on her foot. She screamed and let me go. I lunged for the window.

"Get him!" the captain gasped, but I was already jumping. It was forty feet down—right into the moat. Looks like I was finally getting my bath. I pulled myself out of the water and ran for my life.

The next morning I was on the lam. I hid in an apple tree on Old McDonald's farm, listening to my Walkman. The radio was full of news about me stealing twenty bags of gold from the king's treasury.

I groaned. It was a good scam. The captain was stealing gold from the treasury to convince the king that the miller's daughter could spin straw into gold. With me accused of robbing the treasury, it would be hard to prove that no new gold had been added to it. Instead, the miller's daughter would marry the king, the captain would gain a fortune in stolen gold, and I'd be on my way to the dungeon.

I wanted to scream. I couldn't let the captain get away with this, but what could I do? It would only be a matter of time until the guards found me.

Suddenly it hit me. Actually, it bit me. A horse thrust its head into my tree to nibble an apple and got me instead. I fell out of the apple tree and landed hard on my butt. As I rubbed my bruised leg, I felt something in my pocket that hadn't been there the day before. I pulled it out: a gold coin. How had that gotten in there?

Then I smiled. All at once, I knew how to expose the

captain as a thief, stop the king from marrying a con artist, and clear my name.

The radio said the king's wedding would be that Saturday in the castle. The entire kingdom was invited, and I figured it wouldn't be too hard to sneak in. Nobody would expect that I'd be dumb enough to return to the scene of the crime.

On the wedding day, I hid until the miller and his daughter were marching down the aisle. Then, with a yell I jumped up on the pipe organ. That wedding went quiet faster than Little Bo Peep lost her sheep. The king and his bride were horrified.

The captain of the guard ran toward me.

"You're under arrest, Wrinklesoftskin!" he shouted.

"Rumpelstiltskin!" I yelled. "The name's Rumpel-stiltskin!"

"Whatever," the captain said. Behind him, the wedding guests whispered excitedly. Well, I'd give them even more to whisper about.

"I have come to throw myself on the mercy of Your Majesty," I said, bowing low. "And to restore the stolen gold."

As you can imagine, that got the greedy king's attention. He signaled for silence, then looked at me.

"Very well," he said. "Please tell me where my gold is."

"I'll do better than that; I'll show you."

The captain of the guard started to protest, but the king hushed him. He wanted his gold back. Figuring that he still had the best of me, the captain gave in. Happy came up to tie my hands.

"I can't believe you did it," Happy said with dismay.

"Wait and see," I said. "I might surprise you yet."

Happy finished tying my hands, then dragged me before the king.

"Now," the king said, "lead us to the gold."

I started walking toward the throne room.

"Where are you going?" the king asked.

"The gold's in the castle," I said.

The captain of the guard and the miller's daughter exchanged worried looks, but the king didn't notice. He really wanted his gold back. So I took off, with the king, Happy, the miller and his daughter, and the captain trooping along behind me.

I kept close to the captain. We walked through the throne room, past the treasury, down into the kitchen. The captain was starting to get restless.

"You are trying my patience, Stumblestiltskin," he said.

"The name's . . . oh, never mind," I said. "The gold's nearby; I just forgot which room."

We descended a stairway and walked down a long hall. This was taking longer than I'd thought it would. I was just getting nervous when the captain pulled out a handkerchief, took a deep breath, and sneezed.

"The gold's in there," I said, pointing to the nearest door. It led to the dungeon.

"Preposterous," the captain blustered, but he wasn't in charge here.

"Open the door," the king ordered. Happy marched forward and swung the door wide open. We crowded in to stare at . . . straw. There were piles and piles of straw.

At first no one understood. "Where's the gold?" the king asked. Then Happy smiled, and turned toward the king.

"The captain said all the straw in the kingdom had been turned into gold," Happy said. "If that's true, what's this straw doing here?"

The captain sneezed.

"The miller's daughter didn't spin any straw into gold," I said. "The captain swapped the straw for gold from the treasury, then blamed his theft on me. The two were working in cahoots to rob you, Your Majesty."

"Then where is my gold?" the king asked.

"Hidden in the sewer under the castle," I said. Then I pulled out the gold coin I'd found in my pocket. "I tripped over the bags climbing up here to 'rescue' the miller's daughter, and this slid into my pocket. Then I remembered how the captain smelled like rotten fish the other day—just like I did after crawling through the sewer. I figure he was hiding the gold there until the coast was clear."

The king frowned at the captain and the miller's daughter.

"It wasn't my fault," the miller's daughter stammered. "My father and the captain made me do it."

Well that did it. The miller, his daughter, and the captain began yelling and arguing like you wouldn't believe. There was no honor among these thieves. The king ordered Happy to throw them all in the dungeon. Happy and I then crawled into the sewer and retrieved all the stolen gold.

The next day I came to the castle.

"Congrats on the promotion," I told Happy. He'd been bumped up to captain, what with the former captain doing time.

"Thanks," he said. "Glad to know that you're not a

thief."

"How's the king doing, now that he knows his gold-spinning bride was a fake?"

Happy shrugged. "Actually, he's feeling great. He just heard about this guy named Midas, who has the golden touch. The king thinks he'll be rolling in gold before the week is out."

I groaned. It looked as if the king would be keeping me busy for the next few happily ever afters—very busy. And that's nothing to sneeze at.

The Girl Who Wanted to Be a Princess

BY BRUCE LANSKY

Not long ago, Michelle Koszlowski lived with her parents and her bratty little brother, Donald, in a gray house with white shutters. The Koszlowski house looked just like all the other gray houses with white shutters on Maple Street in Sheboygan, Michigan.

Michelle didn't like her house much. She thought it was too . . . well . . . ordinary. She didn't like cleaning her room, washing the dishes, mowing the lawn, or baby-sitting Donald, either. In fact, she hated any kind of work.

What she did like was hanging out with her friends at the mall and trying on trendy jeans, sneakers, dresses, and tops at her favorite stores. And although Michelle felt embarrassed by her rather ordinary parents, that didn't stop her from begging them for money to enhance her wardrobe.

One day Michelle came down to breakfast wearing a long face, pajamas, and a bathrobe. She slumped heavily into a chair.

"What's the matter, dear?" asked her doting mother.

"I can't possibly go to school today," Michelle pouted, "I have *nothing* to wear."

Her father looked up from his newspaper. "Michelle, honey, please! We can't afford to buy you everything you want. If you want some new clothes, you can earn some money to buy them by helping out around the house: you could mow the lawn or baby-sit your brother."

"Work? Me? You *must* be kidding." Michelle yawned, patting her lips with her hand.

"Get real," joked her mother.

But Michelle did not smile. She scowled as she ate

her breakfast, then, still scowling, she stood up and stomped away from the table.

"You forgot to clear your dishes, Michelle," her mother called after her.

Michelle turned around and stared at her mother. "Why should *I* clear them?

"Because *you* used them," her father exploded. "You must think you're Princess Michelle or something. Well, you're not. You're Michelle Koszlowski, daughter of Joe Koszlowski, a hardworking plumber from Sheboygan."

Michelle glared at her parents. "I wish I *were* Princess Michelle!" she snapped. Then she tossed her head and stalked out of the room, slamming the door behind her.

Michelle's mother looked at her husband and sighed. "Maybe she just wasn't cut out to be a middle-class American kid. Maybe we should tell her the truth—and give her a choice."

Michelle's father nodded grimly.

Michelle's parents found her pouting in her room. "Michelle," her father said solemnly, "there's something you should know." Michelle wiped her eyes and looked up at her father.

"Before World War II, my family lived in Poland," began her father. "The Koszlowskis were titled aristocrats and lived in a centuries-old castle. But when the Communists came to power, the Koszlowskis lost everything. My father moved to America, but his older brother, Alex, and Alex's wife, Lidia, moved to Paris and waited. When the Communists lost the elections in Poland a few years ago, Alex and Lidia moved back to Poland and reclaimed the family property.

"We haven't told you about the old country because we are happy with our life in the United States. But perhaps you aren't. You could visit Poland this summer and stay with Count Alex and Countess Lidia, your great-uncle and great-aunt. They never had children and have always wanted to meet you.

"Of course, their lifestyle is very different from ours. They'd provide you with more new clothes than you could ever wear. You'd never have to clear the table or make your bed. You'd have a butler and maid to serve you. They'd treat you like a princess. You might like it so much, you'd want to stay."

"Yes!" Michelle exclaimed. She had always believed that she deserved the finer things in life. Having lots of clothes and living like a princess in a castle sounded perfect. She was so excited that she blurted out: "There's just a month till summer vacation. I can hardly wait!"

Of course, Michelle's parents were disappointed that she wanted to go, but they loved her very much and wanted her to be happy. Her father called Count Alex and Countess Lidia to ask if they'd like a summer guest. Then Michelle's mother called a travel agent to make arrangements.

Michelle couldn't keep her mind on schoolwork that month. She was too busy daydreaming about her new life and telling all her friends that she'd soon be living in a castle. Her friends clung around her, asking a million questions and calling her Princess Michelle. She loved all the attention.

Finally the school year ended, and Michelle's departure date arrived. The ride to the airport was very sad for Michelle's parents. As Michelle's father hugged her good-bye, he said, "I'm sorry that what we have isn't good enough for you. I hope you will be happy living like a princess. Remember to call home."

Michelle couldn't understand why her parents were so glum, but she indulged them each with a hug and a kiss. No sooner was she on the airplane than her spirits soared. She fell asleep dreaming of life as Princess Michelle. She didn't wake up until the plane landed.

A chauffeur in a dark suit and cap met her at the airport and whisked her away in a sleek black Mercedes with a TV and refrigerator. Soon after she finished a bottle of mineral water and a can of smoked almonds, the car glided through the gates of an old, ivy-covered castle. It looked right out of a fairy tale.

A butler opened the large oak door for her and showed her to her room. A maid ran a bath for her and told her to dress for dinner. Her closet was stocked with elegant clothes that she could tell were far more costly than anything she'd ever seen at the mall. Michelle's great-aunt had spared no expense. It was almost too good to be true!

At dinner Michelle met Count Alex and Countess Lidia, who were dressed in formal evening clothes. They told her how pleased they were to have her with them. "Here you'll have the best of everything, my dear," said Count Alex.

"Of course, you must learn how to behave like a proper young lady," said Countess Lidia. "First, you must learn how to dress for dinner. Please go back upstairs and take off those awful blue jeans and put on something more appropriate. And please remove that bubble gum from your mouth. You look like a cow chewing her cud. It's so uncivilized."

As a farewell gift, Michelle's father had bought her a new pair of jeans for her trip, and Michelle loved them. But she did as she was told. She returned wearing a sophisticated black evening dress and shiny black shoes that had been set out for her by her chambermaid.

"Your education begins tonight. Our meal will begin with escargots, which are snails—a French delicacy," explained Countess Lidia. "The entrée will be sweetbread, which is a fancy name for a calf's pancreas. The third course will be spinach soufflé."

"I'd prefer a hamburger and French fries with plenty of ketchup," said Michelle.

"That's quite out of the question," snapped Countess Lidia. "Go ahead and pick up your little fork, dig the snail out of its shell, and place it in your mouth, young lady." Again Michelle did as she was told, grimacing all the while. "If you insist on making hideous faces," warned Countess Lidia, "you'll be asked to leave the table."

Michelle stopped grimacing, but she didn't eat much of the exotic food set before her.

After dinner Count Alex and Countess Lidia took Michelle on a tour of the castle grounds. Inside there was a huge ballroom illuminated by real crystal chandeliers. Outdoors there were stables and a riding ring filled with jumps of different heights.

"You'll love our horses," Count Alex chatted. "You do ride, don't you?"

"Sure," Michelle said hesitantly. What she didn't say was that trotting nauseated her and the thought of jumping over fences on a horse gave her nightmares.

Michelle searched for a more comfortable topic of conversation. Although the castle was crawling with servants, she had not noticed any children. "Are there any kids my age nearby?" she asked.

"No, but that shouldn't be a problem," the countess replied. "You'll be much too busy with your studies to have time for socializing."

"Studies? In the summer? In Michigan school's out from June through August."

"You won't be going to school," explained Countess Lidia. "We've hired a tutor for you. You have a lot to learn about Polish language, history, and culture. The sooner you get started, the better. Don't you agree?"

Michelle didn't answer. She was thinking about how

much she'd miss all her friends. Her reverie ended when Count Alex announced, "You'll be happy to know that tonight, in honor of your arrival, we're having a special concert of chamber music. I hope you like it."

At seven o'clock, guests began arriving in formal attire to meet "Young Lady Michelle," who was dressed in a stunning white evening gown and the world's most uncomfortable pair of high heels. After another dinner featuring exotic, unfamiliar foods, all the guests were seated in the ballroom for the concert.

Michelle was bored stiff. She couldn't stand classical music and asked to be excused. Countess Lidia gave her a stern look and told her it would be rude to leave. "Sit up straight, like a proper young lady, and stop squirming," she added. Michelle wanted to scream, but instead she sat still, biting her lip with anger.

After the concert, Michelle circulated among the guests, many of whom spoke English. But she soon tired of polite chitchat with stuffy Polish aristocrats about the violinist's "wonderful vibrato" and the "marvelous hors d'oeuvres" and went upstairs to bed.

As Michelle lay in her enormous bedroom, surrounded by portraits of her ancestors, tears rolled from her eyes. She missed her ordinary parents. She missed her friends. She even missed her bratty brother. Michelle cried herself to sleep.

The next morning she was quite hungry. Michelle threw a bathrobe over her pajamas and ran downstairs to the kitchen to look for something to eat.

"Out, out. This is no place for a young lady," said the cook, shooing with her hands.

"But I'm hungry," pleaded Michelle.

"You'll have to wait until breakfast is served," the cook answered sternly. "Your choice of smoked salmon or pickled herring."

"Ish!" moaned Michelle. "I hate fish. I want some corn flakes."

"I'm very sorry, but we don't have any corn flakes," said the cook. "Now please go. Breakfast will be served at nine."

Michelle was hungry. She was frustrated and lonely, too. She picked up a phone and tried to call home, but kept getting an operator who spoke only Polish.

Countess Lidia, dressed in riding clothes, found Michelle sitting next to the telephone with tears in her eyes. "It isn't easy making a phone call if you don't know Polish. That's why you must begin your studies immediately. By the way, whom are you trying to call?"

"I want to call my parents," sobbed Michelle.

"You'll have to wait until afternoon. Right now it's about two in the morning in Michigan," Countess Lidia told Michelle. "In the meantime, I'd like you to change into your riding clothes and then join me for breakfast. After that we'll see what you know about horses."

Michelle was not anxious to show Countess Lidia what she knew about horses, which wasn't much. Nonetheless, she put on her riding clothes and showed up for breakfast at the stroke of nine. She was so hungry, she actually ate a few bites of pickled herring before laying down her fork. She folded her hands in front of her and stared at them grimly as the Countess finished eating.

After breakfast, Michelle learned the proper way to mount a horse, sit in the saddle, and post when the horse trotted. Her seat and knees were quite sore when the lesson ended. Her stomach felt queasy, and her face was white. Michelle dreaded jumping over the fences in the ring, which her riding instructor assured her she would attempt by summer's end.

After a long, hot bath and a change of clothes, Michelle was ready for lunch. She was greeted by a plate full of fried chicken livers, which she didn't touch. If it hadn't been for the black bread, she would have starved.

"What's the matter, Michelle? Aren't you hungry?" asked Countess Lidia. "You're not homesick, are you?"

Well, that did it. Michelle burst into tears. Sobbing uncontrollably, she asked Countess Lidia what time it was in Sheboygan.

"It's about six-forty-five in the morning," answered Countess Lidia.

Michelle's tears stopped flowing as suddenly as they'd started. "Perfect timing!" she exclaimed. "If I call now, I'll catch everyone at home."

So Countess Lidia got the American Koszlowskis on the line, handed the phone to Michelle, and left the room to give her some privacy. Donald was on the other end.

"Hello, Donald!" Michelle said. "How are you? How is your hamster? I miss you both so much!" Donald couldn't believe his ears. For as long as he could remember, Michelle had called him "The Brat" and his hamster "The Rat." She rarely talked to him, unless he was holding the TV remote control and she wanted it.

Soon both her parents got on the line. "How's my

little princess?" her father asked.

Suddenly Michelle began to bawl. "I want to come home," she cried. "I don't want to be a princess any more. I'm sick of dressing for dinner, escargots, pickled herring, servants, riding lessons, sitting up straight, and chamber music. I miss corn flakes, hamburgers with French fries, blue jeans, school, my friends, my mother and father, and even Donald and his hamster. Please let me come home."

"But I thought you'd like all the fancy clothes and servants," offered her mother.

Her father added, "We just don't have enough money to afford all the things you want us to buy."

"That's okay," cried Michelle. "I don't really need all that junk. And if I do want something special, I'll work for it. I really will."

"I'm happy to hear that," said her mother, "because we're going to a PTA meeting tomorrow night, and we'll need a babysitter for Donald."

"I'm going home!" shouted Michelle so loudly that she could be heard in the garden, where Countess Lidia was inspecting her roses, and on the putting green, where Count Alex was practicing his golf game.

"No sooner said, than done," muttered Count Alex.

A servant handed him a cellular phone, and he fired off some orders.

It didn't take long for the butler to pack Michelle's personal belongings and hand them to the chauffeur, who was waiting with the Mercedes at the front door. Michelle jumped into her favorite blue jeans and stuck a huge piece of bubble gum into her mouth. As the car glided out the castle gates, a big smile lit Michelle's face. She couldn't wait to get back to her gray house with white shutters on Maple Street, her ordinary parents, and her bratty brother, Donald.

The Little Tailor

BY TIMOTHY TOCHER

In a little village deep in the forest lived a tailor. His father had been a tailor before him, and his grandfather, too . . . and so on back through the generations. The tailor was a small man, so everyone called him the Little Tailor. He lived alone behind his shop, which sat above a bakery on the main street of the village. While the villagers admired his skill, they didn't enjoy his company because of one really annoying fault: he continually bragged about himself.

The Little Tailor loved his shop. Although the bakery below sometimes made his shop a little too warm, it also filled the place with delicious aromas. In fine weather the Little Tailor often sat on the sill of his large window, sewing, enjoying the breeze, and watching the hustle and bustle of the street below.

Since his work was truly of the highest quality, the Little Tailor was always busy. Today he was sewing new aprons for the baker and the baker's wife. He was eager to finish. He knew the baker would give him a fresh apple tart, his favorite sweet, along with his payment. At last he tied off the last stitch and hurried downstairs.

As the Little Tailor walked in, the baker was sliding the tarts out of the oven. He praised the fine stitching on the new aprons, but not as much as the Little Tailor praised himself.

"Well, Baker, you know I can do a job only one way," the Little Tailor boasted. "A king's robe or a baker's apron, my stitches are always perfect."

"And when has a king ever visited our village?" asked the baker.

"If one did, you know he would seek me out."

With that the Little Tailor accepted a hot, sticky tart and went back upstairs.

He set the tart on the windowsill to cool while he straightened his shop. Humming happily as he worked, he was soon ready for his snack. He approached the window and saw to his dismay that a swarm of flies had discovered the tart. He grabbed a piece of fabric from his worktable and swatted at them.

From either the stickiness of the tart or their full bellies, the flies were slow to react. The Little Tailor was amazed to discover that he had killed seven of them with a single blow. He was so proud of his aim that he scooped up the flies and rushed downstairs to show the baker.

"Look, Baker! Seven with one blow! I know my hands are steady and my eyes sharp, but I never realized the lightning speed I possess! Can you believe it?" As he spoke, he held out the handful of dead flies.

"Don't bring your flies in here!" the baker scolded. "The street boys will be telling everyone they're the raisins in my scones."

"But aren't you amazed? Seven with one blow! Don't you wish your hands were that quick?"

"You'll see how quick my hands are if you don't quit bragging and get rid of those disgusting flies!" thundered the baker.

Reluctantly the Little Tailor stepped outside to drop the flies into the street. The baker's wife was just returning from a delivery.

"Mrs. Baker, come and look! Seven with one blow! Has any man a quicker hand or a keener eye? Let me tell you how it happened."

"Please, Tailor, it's quite enough to hear you brag about your sewing all the time. You're just like our old cat, bringing dead mice to show off."

With that she entered the shop and closed the door. The Little Tailor would not be thwarted. He followed her inside.

"Well, Mrs. Baker, I can understand your jealousy. But it's not bragging if it's the truth. Anyone will tell you I sew the straightest stitches around, and now I've proven that I have the quickest hands as well. Who knows what other talents I might have?"

"And who cares?" retorted the baker. "Go discover your talents so my wife and I can get back to our work."

"Baker, try to control your jealousy. You're a perfectly fine baker. Not everyone can have as many different talents as I do. Why, with my quick hands and my sharp eyes, I could probably go anywhere and do anything."

"Tailor, you've never left this tiny village," said the baker's wife. "You still live in the shop where you were born. There's a big world out there that just might swallow you up if you're not careful."

The Little Tailor was taken back by her bluntness. "I have thought many times about seeing the world," he said. "However, what would this town be without me?"

"It would be a lot more quiet, I warrant."

"Hmph!" snorted the Little Tailor. He wasn't used to such frankness. To salvage his dignity, he announced, "I *will* go out to see the world, then. Perhaps I'll move to the big city. The people of this village clearly do not appreciate my many talents."

The Little Tailor stormed up the stairs to his shop. He gathered some bread and cheese from his larder and wrapped them in a handkerchief. He tied the bundle to a stick and slung it over his shoulder. He then crammed his pockets with packets of needles, spools of thread, a pair of scissors, some thimbles, and a pincushion.

He was about to leave when he spotted the scrap of material with which he had slain the seven flies. He sat on the windowsill one last time and embroidered the words "Seven with one blow" in bright red thread onto the scrap. He then tied it across his chest like a sash, locked up the shop, and left.

The Little Tailor had thought he would travel far before nightfall, but in the forest darkness came early. He had only gone a few miles when he decided he had better stop for the night. He dropped his bundle under a giant oak and sat with his back against the trunk. There he ate his meager dinner and fell asleep.

The Little Tailor awoke stiff and cold to a dewy morning. At first he forgot where he was, but then recalled the unpleasantness of the previous day. He was determined to go on. He hadn't walked far when the ground began to shake. In fear he wrapped his arms around a tree and waited for what he thought was an earthquake to pass.

Instead his unbelieving eyes beheld the approach of a giant as wide as the path and ten feet tall. Swallowing hard, the Little Tailor reminded himself how talented he was. He jumped into the path and shouted, "Stand aside, sir, and make way!"

The startled giant halted and scanned the trail for his challenger. When he saw the bold Little Tailor, he was overcome with laughter.

"You dare to challenge me? Why, my breakfast was bigger than you! Run off while you still can."

"Mind your manners, Giant, and clear the path for a better man," responded the Little Tailor.

At this impudence the giant reached out and scooped up the Little Tailor with one greasy hand. He lifted him to eye level and the Little Tailor felt his hot breath. Whatever the giant had eaten for breakfast had been none too fresh.

The giant was about to toss the Little Tailor into the treetops when he noticed the embroidered sash. "Seven with one blow?" he wondered. "Can this little fellow be tougher than he looks?" Just to be the safe, the giant decided to test the Little Tailor's strength before dealing with him.

He set the Little Tailor down and said, "So you're a mighty man, eh? Let's feel your strongest grip." The giant extended his massive hand. The tailor filled his hand with needles to jab into the giant's flesh as they shook. "Let's see how he likes this grip!" he thought.

But the giant's hands were so tough and callused that the needles bent without piercing his skin. The Little Tailor had to quickly beg for mercy lest his own hand be pierced.

"You don't have much tolerance for pain," laughed the giant. "I barely got hold of you before you gave up."

"No tolerance for pain?" asked the Little Tailor. "Let's see you match this feat!"

With that the Little Tailor whipped out his scissors and stuck them into his own chest. Of course, a pincushion was hidden in his breast pocket.

The giant, however, seemed unimpressed. He pulled out a dagger as long as the Little Tailor's leg and plunged it into his own chest. Although the tailor didn't know it, the giant was carrying half a roasted pig under his jacket in case he needed a snack on the trail.

The Little Tailor winced, but was still not ready to give in. He gathered a handful of nuts from beneath a nearby chestnut tree. He slipped two metal thimbles out of his pocket and hid them among the nuts.

"Let's see you crack this mouthful of nuts with your teeth," the tailor said. He held out his hands to the giant.

Laughing, the giant popped everything in his mouth. He chewed twice and swallowed—nuts, shells, thimbles, and all.

"Now you've whetted my appetite," the giant cried. "I think I'll suck the marrow from this bone, if you'll be so kind as to crack it for me."

The giant pulled a gristly bone from one pocket of his jacket and offered it to the Little Tailor. It was so large, the Little Tailor couldn't open his mouth wide enough to bite it. His tiny teeth scratched feebly at the bone while the giant roared with laughter.

"Seven with one blow! Why, you must have killed seven bugs," roared the giant. "I think I'll see how far I can throw you!"

As the giant reached down, the terrified Little Tailor ran between his legs. He swore, "If I get out of this, I'll never brag again. If not for my boasting, I would be safe and happy in my shop right now."

He then looked up at an ugly sight. The giant's trousers were split in the rear, exposing his none-too-clean underwear. As the giant grabbed him and wound up to throw him over the trees, the Little Tailor had one last desperate idea.

"Giant, if you spare my life, I will repair all your clothes. I am but a humble tailor, yet perhaps I can be of service to you."

His arm cocked, the giant paused. He had never learned how to sew. He had left his parents two years ago and by now every garment he owned was torn.

"Tailor, if I spare your worthless life, will you come live in my cave until all my clothes are repaired? I warn you, it will not be easy work."

"Yes, kind giant, I promise to do whatever you need. Only . . . please . . . let me live."

For two long months the Little Tailor lived in the giant's smelly, drafty cave. He worked from sunrise to sunset mending the giant's shredded clothing. Not only was the giant unable to sew, he had obviously never heard of soap, either. Every garment was filthy and putrid, covered with food and other unidentifiable stains. The tailor was miserable, but he knew his bragging had brought him to this.

Each day as he labored, he dreamed of his little shop and longed to be perched once more on its windowsill. To his surprise, he also remembered how well the people in the village had always treated him, despite his excessive bragging.

At last the day came when the Little Tailor mended the giant's final torn garment. Since it was nearly dark when he tied off the last stitch, he decided to get some sleep before leaving. When he woke up in the morning, he thought, "What a beautiful day." He did not care that the day was actually gray and misty. He was going home, so the day was beautiful.

As he looked around the cave, the Little Tailor saw that the giant was already awake. He stood next to the pile of the mended clothing, inspecting each garment.

"Well," the giant said, "you've upheld your part of the bargain. You are a free man. But if I see you in these parts again, you'd better show good manners. No one should be as rude as you were."

The Little Tailor bowed his head. "I know that now. Here." The Little Tailor reached into his pocket and removed the crumbled sash that said "Seven with one blow." He said, "Take this. I have no use for it anymore."

The giant took the sash and shoved it into one of his newly mended pockets. He then patted the Little Tailor on the back, almost knocking him off his feet. "Well, off with you, then."

The Little Tailor walked quietly out of the cave and turned onto the path that would lead him home. He thought about his beloved shop, his quiet village, his neighbors, and the baker's tarts.

The closer he came to the village, the lighter his steps became. Soon, he was skipping joyfully down the main street of the village. His mouth watered as he approached the bakery and smelled fresh tarts being baked.

As he entered the bakery, the baker and his wife looked up from their work.

"Tailor! We thought you had left us for good," said the wife.

"Where have you been? What adventures did you have?" asked the baker. "You've been gone so long, even your bragging will be a welcome sound."

"Mr. and Mrs. Baker, there will be plenty of time for stories in the years ahead. For now, I'll say only that I'm happy to be back and glad to see your friendly faces again. I guess I had to leave this place to realize how good it is."

"But aren't you upset because we don't appreciate your many talents?" asked the baker's wife.

"I was wrong." the Little Tailor humbly replied. "This village is perfect for me."

The baker and his wife looked at each other and smiled. Whatever adventures the Little Tailor had experienced seemed to have done him a lot of good.

"Would you like to eat some fresh tarts with us?" the baker asked, pulling a piping hot tray of tarts out of the oven.

"Please," said the Little Tailor. "And if any flies try to eat my tart this time, I think I'll just shoo them away."

A Thoroughly Modern Rapunzel

(Or How I Outsmarted the Witch)

BY JUDE MANDELL

So there I was, me—Rapunzel—prisoner in a tall apartment building, grounded for life by an evil witch . . . all because my mom was crazy about pizza!

Here's how it all began. There was once a witch named Mesmerelda who sold the tastiest pizzas in New York. Her recipe was a secret blend of tomatoes, toad toes, spices, spiders, cheese, crust, and magic spells. One bite and you were hooked.

Mom and Dad lived in a tiny house next to

Mesmerelda's restaurant. My father was out of work, so they were too poor to buy her pizza. But they were happy. They were going to have a child: me.

"Youse two lovebirds are lucky," Mesmerelda said when she heard the news. "I always wanted a brat of my own."

The next day, a free sample of Mesmerelda's Magically Delicious Pizza appeared on my parents' doorstep. A mouth-watering smell drifted from the box.

Mom tasted a slice first. One bite and she was hooked. The next thing Dad knew, she'd wrestled him to the ground and snatched his slice, too.

"Get a grip!" he said, as she shoved both slices in her mouth. "I would have given you my slice if you'd asked."

"Sorry," said Mom. "It's like some weird spell hit me."

From that day on, Mom was nuts for Mesmerelda's pizza. When the aroma wafted in from next door, drool dribbled down her chin. Soon she refused to eat anything else.

My father scraped together as much money as he could to buy pizza for my mom, but he could never buy as much as she wanted. So one night when everyone was asleep, my worried father sneaked into

Mesmerelda's kitchen. He quickly grabbed a pizza, stripped off the anchovies, and crept toward the door.

Five steely fingers grabbed his arm. "What's da matter, thief? Ya don't like anchovies?" shouted Mesmerelda.

"Don't sneak up like that," Dad yelled. "You almost gave me a heart attack."

"Wait till I call da cops, and dey throw you in jail," said the witch. "Dat won't be too good for your health, either."

"I'll pay you for the pizza when I get a job, Mesmerelda. Think of it as a loan."

"Yo! Do I look like a bank? Hand it over, thief."

"But my wife will starve without your pizza! She won't eat anything else!"

"Well, I wouldn't want dat to happen, her havin' da kid and all," Mesmerelda said. "Tell you what. Your wife gets all da pizza she wants, on one condition—I get da brat when it's born."

"Trade our baby for pizzas?" said Dad. "No way! How's about I wash your pizza pans instead and work off what I owe?"

"No dice! No baby, no pizza!"

Dad considered. Surely he could change Mesmerelda's mind by the time I was born. "All right," he said. "My wife's favorite is pizza topped with rapunzel salad."

Mesmerelda grinned. "One rapunzel special comin' up!"

As the months went by, Dad had no luck in getting Mesmerelda to change her mind.

"Nope!" she'd say. "Da only way you can pay me off is in baby-bucks."

The minute I wailed my way into the world, Mesmerelda leaped in the window and snatched me from my mother's arms.

"A girl-brat!" she said. "Thanks. I'll call her Rapunzel." She threw some half-price pizza coupons on the bed. "Here's a bonus, youse two. Enjoy!"

Dad ran after her. "No! You can't take our daughter," he cried. "We'll sell everything we own to pay you back!"

"Youse two are gettin' on my nerves," said Mesmerelda.

With a flick of her magic pizza cutter, she changed both my parents into pizza-delivery vans. She jumped into one of them and drove me to a tall apartment building in a deserted neighborhood. She then sealed the windows and doors with magic spells so only she could get in and out.

Every day, she fed me pizza sauce in baby bottles, pizza-flavored baby food, and, when I grew teeth, regular pizza. Eating nothing but pizza made my hair grow like crazy. It was about a jillion feet long by the time I turned seven.

"Seven years old today, eh? You're growin' fast, Rapunzel," said Mesmerelda. "Though you ain't really my kid, I'm countin' on you to run my pizza place when I get old. Someday it'll be yours."

"What?" I said. "You mean you're not my mother?"

"Get real," she said. "We ain't exactly look-alikes."

I pleaded with her to tell me what had become of my parents. When she told me about the delivery vans, I got very upset. Afraid I might run away, she moved me to the top floor of the building and removed all the staircases, inside and out.

"Yo, Rapunzel!" she'd yell when she came to visit. "Let down your hair. Pizza delivery."

I'd throw my long braids over the balcony. Up she would climb, pizza box under her arm.

I put up with this craziness until my thirteenth birthday, when I blew out all the candles on my cake-and-ice-cream pizza and said, "My wish is to be like the kids I see on TV. I want to have friends, go to school, and eat something besides pizza—hot dogs, bagels, tuna-on-rye. If you don't promise I can do these things, I'll never let my hair down to you again!"

"Talk back to me, will ya?" she screeched.

She picked up her magic pizza cutter. The next thing I knew, I was a giant pepperoni sausage with long hair. The spell lasted a month. After that, I knew I had to escape.

A week later, a young guy came hip-hopping by the apartment building, his boom box blaring. I stared. No one ever came here. I whistled to him through my teeth, yelled, and stamped my feet. He didn't hear, so I grabbed the nearest pizza and hurled it like a Frisbee.

It hit him—*smack!*—in the face.

"Hey!" he yelled. "What's the big idea?"

"Sorry," I shouted, "but I need your help."

He scraped the spinach-and-peanut-butter pizza off his face and got a good look at me. Off went the boom box. "No problemo, beautiful," he said. "You can throw pizza at me anytime."

"Rapunzel, Rapunzel!" called a familiar voice.

"Hide!" I said. "Here comes the witch who keeps me captive." The guy ducked into the alley just before Mesmerelda appeared.

"Yo, Rapunzel! Pizza delivery!" she cried.

I let down my long locks. Up climbed Mesmerelda.

As soon as she left, the guy climbed up. He found me scratching my scalp. "Cooties?" he asked, backing away.

"No!" I said, insulted. "All that pulling on my hair makes my scalp itch."

He came closer and helped me scratch. "Why doesn't the witch just fly up here on her broom?"

"She doesn't have a broom," I said. "Besides, flying makes her throw up."

"Sorry I asked," he said. "My name's Doug Toto. You old enough to date, Rapunzel? You like to dance?"

"One step at a time," I said. "First, I need your help to escape from this boring apartment." I nibbled a piece of pizza.

"Got that figured out already," he said. "Be ready to leave at daybreak."

That night Mesmerelda took so long climbing up my hair, my scalp itched worse than ever.

"Darn it, Mesmerelda," I complained, too irritated to think about what I was saying. "Why do you take so long to climb my hair? Doug Toto climbs it as fast as a spider."

Mesmerelda dropped the goat-cheese-and-zucchini

pizza she was holding. "What are you talkin' about?"

I realized too late what I had revealed. "Nothing," I said.

"Nuttin'? Rapunzel, you got more hair den brains. You want I should turn you into a giant mushroom dis time? Tell me about dis boyfriend of yours."

I could never escape my prison if I were a giant mushroom. Sighing, I told her everything.

Mesmerelda's eyes flashed. "So dis guy, Doug Toto, is tryin' to break you out, eh?" she said. "We'll see about dat!" She climbed back down my hair. When she reached the ground, she pulled out her magic pizza cutter and waved it at me.

Suddenly I felt strangely light-headed. "Oh no!" I wailed.

At the crack of dawn, I heard Doug's voice calling, "Rapunzel, Rapunzel, let down your hair!"

I stuck my head out the window.

Doug took a step backward. "Good grief," he said. "You're as bald as a bowling ball!"

"Well, doesn't *that* make me feel attractive!" I snapped.

"I meant a very pretty bowling ball. Relax, Rapunzel. Your hair will grow back."

"Not soon enough for you to climb up it and rescue me. Mesmerelda will be here soon with my bacon-and-eggs pizza." I was thinking more clearly now that I had more brains than hair.

"Darn it!" he said. "I brought ropes to tie to the balcony so we could climb down together. But I was counting on using your hair to get up there."

"Let's have some cold pizza and think of another plan," I said. I took a piece and tossed the rest of the leftover goat-cheese-and-zucchini pizza, box and all, down to him. It hit the ground with a thud.

"Really, Rapunzel," said Doug. "Don't you know littering is a bad habit?"

I stared down at the thousands of other pizza boxes I had thrown from my balcony day after day and year after year. I began to smile. "Not in my case," I said.

An hour later, Mesmerelda bounced up onto the balcony on her new jet-powered pogo stick. But Doug and I had already climbed down the staircase of pizza boxes he'd built.

Mesmerelda spotted us running. "I'll get you, my pretty," she screeched. "You and your little Doug Toto!"

She jumped on her pogo stick and bounced after us. *Boink! Boink!*

"Faster, Doug!" I cried. "She's gaining on us."

As we raced out of sight, Mesmerelda screeched with rage and shifted the pogo stick into hyperdrive.

Instead of moving forward, she blasted up until she was almost flying. "Oh no!" she gasped. "Flying makes me sick." As she tried to stop herself from throwing up, she lost her grip on the pogo stick and plummeted down, hitting the street at a hundred miles an hour.

A Mesmerelda's Pizza delivery van flattened what was left of her. A second later the van turned into a man. Way to go, Dad!

My hair never grew back. That made me so mad, I never wanted to see another Mesmerelda's Pizza again. My parents and I sold the pizza place to a guy named Hansel and his sister, Gretel. They were nice, but kind of weird about witches and ovens.

Oh, yes . . . I finally enrolled in school—the same one Doug went to—and my new hairstyle made me the coolest girl in class. And the best thing was, I never had to worry about having a bad hair day.

The Fairy Godfather

BY LIYA LEV OERTEL

Have you ever heard of a fairy godfather? Nope? Well, it's no surprise. For centuries, men weren't allowed to be fairy godmothers.

The Director of the Fairy Academy would not even consider applications from men. "They will mess everything up," she said. "What do men know about matchmaking, dancing, or the latest fashions? We fairy godmothers are doing just fine. Why change a system that works?"

Well, I was determined to become a fairy godfather. I wanted to help people. The Academy had a long waiting list of folks who needed assistance with everything from removing warts to finding spouses. Besides, fairy godmothers looked really cool with their long sparkly robes, fairy dust, and magic wands.

My aunt Matilda knew the Fairy Director and had once done her a favor, so the Fairy Director owed her. I convinced Aunt Matilda to call in her favor. The Fairy Director swallowed her disapproval and accepted me into the Academy.

In general, I enjoyed my classes. I learned all sorts of useful stuff: how to comfort distressed damsels, convince uncooperative princes, hoodwink evil stepmothers, get fairy dust out of clothes, and so on.

However, a few things didn't make sense to me. We were taught to create the most uncomfortable and complicated clothing, hair styles, and footwear possible for the ladies we helped. How can anyone live happily ever after if everything—from the hair to the shoes—pinches, constricts, and squishes?

"Why can't women wear comfortable flat shoes?" I asked the Fairy Director. "Why should we give them high-heeled shoes that are a size too small?"

The director sighed loudly and rolled her eyes. Impatiently she explained, "High heels make the legs look longer, and smaller shoes make the feet look dainty. Such shoes also prevent unladylike gallivanting."

"What's wrong with loose hair and ponytails?" I asked. "Why must young ladies wear hairdos so big they can barely fit through doorways?"

The Fairy Director looked like she had a toothache. "Such hair styles make the neck look slimmer," she answered through clenched teeth. "Besides, the more elaborate the hair style, the less the young lady can move around. She is forced to sit quietly, looking elegant and helpless. Princes like that."

"Why can't we create roomy clothes instead of stuffing ladies into corsets?" I asked. "And what's with all these lifeless colors? How about some lively blue or bright red—something fun?"

The Director clenched her fists and tried to keep her cool. "That's rather obvious, I should think. The tighter the dress, the more fragile the young lady looks. The colors she wears should emphasize the lady's pallor and make her look a little sick—to play the sympathy angle."

"Okay," I said. "But—"

"No more stupid questions!" fumed the Director. "That's the way things are. Learn it or leave!"

I bit my tongue. It was clear I could do nothing to change the Academy. "That's okay," I thought. "Once I graduate, I can talk some sense into the young ladies themselves."

The Academy's final exam consisted of a written test and a field test. The written part was a breeze; I knew what the Fairy Director expected, and I gave it to her. The field test was a different story. I vowed to stick to my principles and liberate some young lady from the straightjacket of tradition.

I was given a magic wand, a pouch of fairy dust, and the name of the young lady I was to help. I was excited about revolutionizing the fairy-godmother profession. However, I soon learned that my revolution wasn't going to be easy.

Millie, my assigned damsel in distress, didn't even want to talk to me. As I zapped myself into her bedroom, a pillow smacked me in my face. When I regained my balance, I looked around and saw Millie peeking at me from behind a dresser.

"Who are you?" Millie screamed. "What are you doing in my room? Help!"

"I am here to help you," I said soothingly. "I am your fairy godfather."

"Yeah, right," she said suspiciously. "I requested a fairy god*mother*."

Eventually I convinced Millie of my good intentions and talked her out from behind the dresser. She described the outfit she wanted me to create for her.

"Are you sure you want to wear a tight dress?" I asked. "You'll hardly be able to breathe, let alone dance or eat all the great desserts you'll find at the ball. How about a nice loose jumper?"

"What kind of fairy godfather are you?" Millie cried. "You're supposed to make me beautiful. Who cares about breathing? I can breathe tomorrow."

"How about a comfy pair of loafers," I asked, "instead of vise-grip stilts? You could dance all night and even walk home if the evening is nice."

"Loafers!" Millie exclaimed with horror. "My feet are supposed to look dainty. So what if I have blisters for weeks? I'll take footbaths."

"That pond-scum green makes you look sick," I said, trying to reason with her as she held up a fabric sample to her face. "How about a lovely purple, which would really bring out your eyes?"

"Purple!" Millie almost fainted. "No one wears purple anymore. My *mother* wore purple. This green is the color of the season and I *have* to wear it!"

And so it went. I stuck to my principles, but Millie simply wouldn't listen to reason. She missed the ball, and someone else got the prince. She cried herself to sleep and then wrote a long letter to the Fairy Director.

The Fairy Director called me into her office.

"You are an embarrassment to the Academy," she said, not even bothering to hide her delight. "You failed your field test miserably. We cannot allow you to work with people. But I am not cold-hearted." She smiled sweetly. "I will give you another chance . . . if you complete a special project."

"I would be happy to prove myself," I said eagerly. "What type of project?"

"Oh, it's nothing difficult," she assured me innocently. "You will go from pond to pond, from forest to forest, and find all the enchanted frogs. You will then break their spells. It should take you no longer than a hundred years." She was so pleased, she looked like a wolf who had eaten the three pigs and the three little goats.

I stared at her, hoping she was kidding. "Do you have any idea how many frogs there are in the world?" I asked.

"A lot," she answered, rubbing her hands gleefully. "A whole lot."

And so I went, looking for the rare enchanted frogs among the millions of amphibians in the world. During the next hundred years, I found three enchanted frogs and managed to hook each one up with a princess. It wasn't easy—not many princesses are willing to kiss a frog, even if it is enchanted.

Finally my project was finished and I returned to the Academy. "A few things have changed since you were last among humans," the Fairy Director told me. "But I don't have time to explain. Here is the address of a young lady, Cindy, who has a problem. Go, and don't mess this up. This is your last chance."

No pressure, right? I dusted off my magic wand, and *poof!* I stood before a door with a sign that read: "Cindy's room. Keep out. And that means you."

I pushed the door open and peered inside. Cindy was sitting at her desk, her back to the door. Seemed safe enough, although I couldn't understand why she was dressed in pants, like a boy. Well, the Fairy Director did say a few things had changed.

I walked quietly into the room, assumed a dramatic pose—shoulders back, head up, wand raised high—

and cleared my throat to get her attention. "Ahem."

Cindy jumped out of her chair. "Hey! How did you get past the security alarm? And what's with the getup? Halloween was months ago."

I couldn't understand most of what she said, but I was undaunted. "Hello, my dear. I am your fairy godfather, and I understand that you have a problem. I am here to help. Are you pining for a prince? Do you need some pretty things to wear to a ball?"

"Ahaaa," she said, inching toward the door. "Did you escape from a mental institution or something?"

"Why, no, my dear, I am here to help you meet the prince of your dreams. Are you missing a ball? What size gown do you wear? Do you prefer pearls or diamonds? Hair up or down? Two- or three-inch heels?" I whipped out my measuring tape.

"Whoa there," Cindy said, stopping me. "Keep that away from me. I am perfectly happy in my jeans and sweatshirt, and I don't want to go to any ball. So you run along like a good little lunatic, and I won't have to call the police."

I sat down. My head was spinning. Jeans? A girl who didn't want to go to a ball? What in the world was going on? I must have looked very upset, because

Cindy softened up and we had a long talk. She filled me in on the developments of the last hundred years: cars, television, jeans, rock and roll, Rollerblades, everything. After I regained my wits, I decided I liked what I'd heard.

"Okay," I said. "So you're not a helpless damsel. But still, I was sent here to help. If you don't want to go to a ball, what is the problem?"

"Oh yeah," Cindy said. "I'm the president of the Big Brother/Big Sister program at my school—you know, an older kid mentors a younger kid who might be from a poor family or just has one parent. The two spend time together, so the kid has another good role model and someone to trust.

"It's a great program," Cindy continued, "but we don't have enough money to do all the stuff we want to do, like taking the kids to fun places."

"How can I help?" I asked.

"Well," Cindy explained, "I'm trying to plan a fundraiser, and I have only one week left to think of something fun enough to make folks part with their money but cheap to set up."

"H'mm." I scratched my head. "I'm not sure all those fashion classes I took will be of any help here."

Cindy's eyes began to sparkle. "What a great idea! We'll have a fashion show with an entrance fee! You can do cool clothes, can't you?"

"Well, I know how to create oodles of gowns and high heels and . . ."

"No! Nothing lame like that," Cindy exclaimed impatiently. "We'll need *cool* stuff. Jeans. Hiking boots. Funky T-shirts and short fuzzy sweaters. Bright colors. Sneakers of all kinds."

I felt like I was waking from a hundred-year-long sleep. This project was right up my alley. I waved my wand and *poof!* I was wearing jeans and a sweatshirt that said "Fairy Godfathers Rule."

"Wow!" Cindy was impressed. "What else can you do?"

I shrugged modestly. "I guess I could do whatever you like. Where shall we start?"

Cindy pulled a stack of magazines from under her bed—*Seventeen, Teen People, YM*—all magazines for young people. "We'll start here."

We got to work: platform boots, army boots, sling backs, mules, high tops, wide jeans, bleached jeans, colored jeans, jeans with holes, jeans with pockets, jeans with zippers, shorts, cutoffs—we were only on the bottom half, and Cindy's room looked like a clothing warehouse!

Cindy was so excited, she was almost doing cartwheels. "This is fabulous! We will have the best fundraiser ever!"

I completely agreed. I couldn't remember the last time I had so much fun.

Finally Cindy said, "We'd better stop for tonight. It's late, and I have classes early. Tomorrow we'll do tops, then jackets and coats the next day, and hats the day after that—I love hats! I'll take care of publicity. Then we'll set up in the auditorium. I'll tell the rest of the group to meet us there, and we'll all decorate and select models."

Everything went according to plan. The auditorium looked great. The models strutted their stuff, the people poured in, and the money poured out of their pockets. My clothes were a hit.

Cindy spread the word, and my services were constantly in demand. Naturally, I got my diploma—with honors. Best of all, I took over as Director of the Fairy Academy because the old Director refused to keep up with the times. In return for all she'd done for me—or rather, *to* me—I gave her a very special project. It did not require working with people, and she got to spend all her time near ponds, rivers, and lakes—enjoying the great outdoors! I bet you can guess what the project was!

The Clever Princess Who Slept on a Pea

BY DEBRA TRACY

There was once a fair prince who had reached marrying age. He wanted to wed a princess who was not only beautiful to look at, but also beautiful on the inside. He searched far and wide for such a princess, but to no avail.

The prince was in despair, for he deeply desired the companionship of a wife, and he wasn't getting any younger. Even so, he wouldn't settle for just anyone.

Then one stormy evening, a young woman wrapped in a cloak and hood approached the castle.

She was dripping wet and trembling with cold. She told a guard that she was a princess from a distant land, and he immediately took her to see the king.

The king was dining with his family when the young woman was presented to him. "Please remove your hood and let us see you," the king requested.

When the visitor removed her hood and cloak, the prince gasped. She was the most captivating woman he had ever seen; a beauty with long black hair, golden eyes, and creamy brown skin. Her white silk robe was embroidered with purple and gold.

"What is your name?" the king asked.

"I am Princess Mia," the woman answered in a rich, fluid voice.

"How is it that you are so far from home?" the king asked.

"I am on a tour," the princess replied, "to study the ways of people in other lands, so that I may use this knowledge when I rule as queen."

The king and his son were impressed. The princess was not only beautiful; she was also wise. The queen didn't share their enthusiasm, however. Everyone was ignoring her and gaping at the princess.

Just then a maid entered carrying a tray of puddings. She slipped on the wet marble as she neared the princess, and pudding splattered Mia's white silk robe.

"You clumsy oaf!" the queen shouted.

"Forgive me, my lady," the maid stammered, trembling with fear. She grabbed a napkin and tried to wipe the mess away.

Princess Mia placed a gentle hand on the maid's shoulder and, smiling kindly, said, "Don't worry. It was just an accident. My robe can be washed."

The king looked at his son. Admiration shone in the young man's blue-green eyes. The king couldn't help admiring Princess Mia himself. She was not only wise, she was gentle and kind as well. The princess excused herself and left the room to change into a clean robe. When she returned, the king said, "Please continue with your story."

"My entourage and I were on our way home from the tour when lightning struck nearby. The horses reared, and I fell out of my carriage. I tumbled down a small hill as the horses galloped away. In all the commotion, no one realized I had fallen out. As soon as my attendants discover I am missing, they will send a search party for me."

The royal family invited the princess to stay with

them, and the king dispatched scouts to locate her entourage and inform them that the princess would be staying at their castle. As the days went by, the prince and princess fell in love. When they strolled through the royal gardens, talking about their lives and their interests, bubbly laughter filled the air. Princess Mia's merry disposition cheered everyone but the queen.

One evening the prince burst into his parents' quarters with an announcement: "I wish to ask for Princess Mia's hand in marriage."

The king readily consented. But the queen had been jealous of Mia since the moment she had arrived. "I am not convinced that she is a princess," the queen declared.

The prince's face flushed with indignation, and the king's jaw dropped. "How can Mia prove to you that she is a princess?" inquired the king.

The queen was caught off guard. Thinking quickly, she said, "My grandmother, Queen Lucille, said there was only one way to prove if a young woman was of royal blood. A dried pea is placed beneath twenty mattresses piled high on a bed. The young woman in question must sleep atop the mattresses. If she is truly of royal blood, the pea will keep her awake all night."

"That's the most ridiculous thing I've ever heard!"

the prince protested.

"Yes, it is ridiculous," agreed the king. "Nevertheless, if it is your mother's wish, we will try it."

The maid who had spilled pudding on the princess was tending the king and queen's fireplace and overheard the plan. To repay the princess for her kindness, the maid found her and quickly disclosed what she'd heard.

Her cheeks aflame, Princess Mia said, "Thank you for warning me. When I am married to the prince, I will request that you be my personal attendant." Beaming, the maid hurried off.

Princess Mia paced her room as she considered her options. In the morning she could tell the royal family that she'd had the worst night's sleep of her life . . . but why lie to perpetuate such a ridiculous myth? Surely she could come up with a better idea. Finally, she did.

Smiling slyly, she removed a beautiful sapphire pendant from around her neck. When she was traveling, Princess Mia kept this jewel concealed beneath her robes. She stole down the corridor to the queen's private chamber and slipped the pendant under the queen's mattress. Then she strolled calmly to the garden to meet the prince for their evening stroll.

When Princess Mia returned to her room, her bed had been transformed into a tower of mattresses.

"This is how you are to sleep tonight," the queen said imperiously as she swept into the room. "There isn't a more comfortable bed in the castle."

"Thank you, Your Majesty," the princess replied graciously. "I'm sure even your bed couldn't be any more comfortable." Her golden eyes twinkling, she climbed a ladder to the top mattress and sank into her downy nest.

The next morning, Princess Mia entered the royal dining hall fresh-faced and chipper. "Good morning, Your Majesty, Your Majesty, and Your Young Highness," she said to her hosts. Turning to the queen, she added, "And how did you sleep last night, my lady?"

"I had the best night's sleep of my life," lied the queen. In fact, she had been up all night wondering about the princess. "And you, my dear? How did you sleep?" the queen asked.

"Oh, I slept like a baby!" the princess replied.

"Aha!" exclaimed the queen, smiling triumphantly at her husband and son. "Then she isn't a princess after all!"

The prince smoldered. He didn't believe in his mother's ridiculous test. But what could he do?

The king sighed. "I suppose you were right, my

queen, but I must say that I wish it weren't so."

Feigning ignorance, Princess Mia innocently gazed at the queen and said, "Your Majesty, I want to give you a gift for your thoughtful hospitality. I've been waiting for the right time to present it to you. Until now, I've kept it hidden in a place where I knew it would be safe. If you follow me, I will get it for you."

The queen was surprised, flattered, and curious. The queen, king, and prince followed Princess Mia, who led them to the queen's own private chamber.

"Please forgive me," the princess said, "for hiding my treasure in your chamber, but what better place to hide a gift than right under the nose of the receiver?"

Princess Mia smiled coyly, reached beneath the queen's mattress, and pulled out a long gold chain. From it dangled the most brilliant sapphire the royal family had ever seen.

"Mother!" exclaimed the prince. "You slept all night on just one mattress and you never felt the sapphire? It's bigger than fifty peas!"

The blood drained from the king's face. "My dear," he said weakly, "perhaps you are not a real queen."

The queen's face grew red. "Why, of course I am ... I mean ... Well, you see ..." She threw up her arms in resignation. "My grandmother, Queen Lucille, was a little crazy. That pea story must have been an idea she cooked up. I doubted myself that there was anything to it."

The king exhaled in relief. "Yes, yes, my dear. That explains it. You are a real queen, and Mia is a real princess."

Mia winked at the prince. He smiled back approvingly. His beloved was clever, too!

And the queen, after studying the sapphire, changed her mind about the princess. Mia would make a fine daughter-in-law after all.

The king sent a messenger to Princess Mia's family to invite them for a visit. When they arrived, the prince asked for Mia's hand in marriage. They wed shortly thereafter. The celebration was grand, as most royal weddings are. But most eye-catching of all was the exquisite sapphire pendant worn by the queen. Every time the queen glanced at it, she blushed, and looked upon her new daughter-in-law with respect.

The Gold Ring

BY RITA SCHLACHTER

Once upon a time, a nobleman and his wife lived in a large, beautiful manor on the edge of a forest. The couple had a son, whom they named Elton. The nobleman and his wife taught their son to love the land they lived on: the glades and the woods, the streams and the meadows. They also taught him how to ride a horse, and the three spent many happy afternoons together, galloping across the fields and forest trails.

Sadly, when Elton was still but a boy, his mother became very ill and died. The nobleman grieved for three years and raised his son as best he could. Finally, he decided that his son needed a mother and he remarried.

His second wife was a greedy, ill-tempered woman. Before the wedding, she hid her true nature behind a sweet smile, a pleasing manner, and a false concern for Elton. Her son, Miles, was as unpleasant as she. Miles broke Elton's toys and hid Elton's homework to get him in trouble with the tutor. Whenever Miles broke something or picked a fight, he blamed Elton, and Miles's mother always took her son's side. The two made Elton's life miserable.

After a few years, the nobleman also became deathly ill. He summoned Elton and gave him his wedding ring from his first marriage, telling his son not to forget his parents. The nobleman also called his wife and bade her to be good to Elton. A few days later, the nobleman died.

Elton's stepmother lost no time in kicking him out of the house to live and work in the stable. The only thing of value Elton managed to take with him was the gold ring his father had given him. And that was only because his stepmother had not seen it on his finger.

As a nobleman's son, Elton was not used to hard work. But Isaac, the old stable hand, soon taught him how to clean the stables and care for the horses. Since Elton had always loved horses, he did not mind his new life. In fact, he preferred it to living in the big house with his nasty stepmother and stepbrother.

Elton spent most of his time outdoors and the sun turned his skin a deep tan. Isaac and Elton became good friends. Elton was the son Isaac had never had, and he lovingly taught and cared for the boy. In turn, Elton willingly took over the heaviest tasks, making the job easier for the aging Isaac. And so the years passed as Elton grew into a strong, handsome young man.

One afternoon while exercising a horse in the woods, Elton came upon a young lady. The lady was wearing a sky-blue riding habit trimmed in black, and she had the loveliest smile Elton had ever seen.

"My lady, you look troubled," Elton called out. "Can I help you in any way?"

"I was daydreaming instead of watching where I was going," the beautiful stranger replied. "Now I fear I am hopelessly lost."

"I'm quite familiar with the woods," Elton said, smiling. "Tell me where you live, and I will show you the way."

"I'm Lady Ashley from Sandborne Castle." Her voice was as lovely as her smile.

Elton knew the castle. Her father was a wealthy lord. "Sandborne Castle is only a few miles to the east. Follow me."

Elton was in no hurry to leave the lady's company, so he kept his horse to a leisurely walk. Although he was a son of a nobleman equal in social stature and wealth to Lady Ashley's father, he couldn't think of showing up at her door as the simple stable hand he was now. So he savored this brief time with her. Lady Ashley was easy to talk to. Besides riding, she liked working on tapestries and dancing.

All too soon they reached the edge of the woods.

"Sandborne Castle is straight ahead," Elton said sadly. "You can see one of its banners from here."

"Thank you," Lady Ashley said, still smiling. "I don't know what I would have done without your help."

As she galloped off, the black silk scarf around her neck came untied. It fluttered through the air as gracefully as a bird in flight. Elton rode forward and caught it before it touched the ground. Lady Ashley was now a small blue speck in the distance. She would never hear his call, and he would never catch up to her before she reached the castle.

When Elton returned home, he told Isaac all about his chance meeting with Lady Ashley. He hung the silk scarf on a peg in the stable, and every time he looked at it, he remembered their ride. How wonderful things could be if his stepmother hadn't turned him into a stable hand!

Several weeks later, Isaac came into the stable whistling a merry tune. "I know how you can see Lady Ashley again," he announced to Elton.

"How?" Elton dropped the pitchfork he'd been using.

"I just heard that Lady Ashley's father is having a ball at the end of the week. Why, you could even dance with the young lady."

"Do you think I can just walk through the front gate like everyone else?" Elton demanded.

"I do." Isaac's eyes twinkled with merriment.

"Then you must have told my fairy godmother to fly by and change these simple clothes into something suitable for a ball."

"All you need is this." Isaac pulled the silk scarf from the peg. "It's a masquerade ball. There will be highwaymen, pirates, and knights, and I know of at least one stable hand." Isaac took out his knife and cut two slits in the black scarf. "This will be your mask."

"Are you sure this will work?" Elton asked.

"It will work if you remember to leave before the clock chimes twelve."

"What happens then?"

"Everyone unmasks," Isaac answered.

"I'll remember," said Elton.

The next day, Elton learned that Miles was also planning to attend the masquerade ball. Elton overheard his stepmother speaking to Miles in the garden.

"Dress as a swashbuckling pirate or a debonair musketeer, dear Miles," the stepmother instructed her son. "I understand that Lady Ashley is of marrying age. And her family is very rich."

The mere thought of Miles dancing with Lady Ashley made Elton feel sick. "Well, Miles will have one advantage," he thought. "His face will be covered by a mask, so Lady Ashley won't be able to see how mean-spirited he is."

Finally, the night of the masquerade ball arrived. Elton had no trouble entering the castle along with the other masked quests. The black scarf hid his face; only his blue eyes peered through the slits.

Hundreds of candles lit the hall. Tables were laden with delicious food. Red and white roses scented the air. Elton noticed none of these things. He had eyes only for Lady Ashley. She was dressed as a snow queen. Her flowing white gown was covered with silver snowflakes that sparkled in the candlelight. Although she wore a white mask, she gave herself away by instructing the servants in their tasks.

Many young men disguised as kings, minstrels, explorers, and hunters asked Lady Ashley to dance. Then Elton spotted Miles masquerading as a knight with a chain-mail hood concealing his face. Elton had seen Miles leave the house, so he knew what costume Miles had chosen. Just as Miles approached Lady Ashley to ask her to dance, Lady Ashley's glance fell on Elton. She smiled, curtsied, and extended her gloved hand, inviting Elton to be her partner.

"There's something so familiar about you," she said. "Have we met before?"

"Perhaps," answered Elton. As he took her hand, she glanced down at his fingers. Suddenly, Elton wished he'd worn a pair of work gloves with his stable-hand "costume." He sensed that she'd noticed his skin was tanned from the sun and callused from hard work, unlike the hands of a true nobleman. No nobleman would work in the stables as Elton did.

But then Lady Ashley smiled and touched the black silk scarf that covered Elton's eyes. "I used to have a scarf just like that one," she said. "I can't wait until midnight to see you unmasked."

The rest of the evening, Elton and the snow queen danced and talked and danced again. They found that they had much in common and they made each other laugh over and over.

Hours flew by like minutes, and suddenly the clock's chimes burst through the silver-toned notes of the orchestra. *Ten. Eleven. Twelve.* Elton had forgotten to watch the time.

"I must go," he exclaimed.

Lady Ashley was surprised by her partner's sudden urge to leave. "Who are you?" She grabbed Elton's hand, but he pulled free, leaving her holding his ring. "Stop him!" Lady Ashley called out.

Elton dashed for the door, zigzagging around the guards who tried to stop him. He ran down the front steps and disappeared into the darkness.

The next day, word spread quickly about the mysterious guest for whom Lady Ashley was combing the countryside. Elton overheard his stepmother telling Miles that, according to rumors, Lady Ashley wanted to marry the mysterious stranger.

Two weeks later, Lady Ashley and her escort came to the manor Elton once called home. His stepmother and Miles rushed out to greet her. The escort explained that the Lady's favorite dance partner at the ball had left suddenly, leaving behind only his ring. She was searching for the owner of the ring.

Lady Ashley slipped the ring onto Miles's finger. It was a perfect fit. His mother was overjoyed. She shrieked, "It fits! It fits!" and clapped her hands.

Then Lady Ashley looked at Miles's pale, soft hands. "But the ring cannot be yours," she protested.

"It is! It is!" Elton's stepmother screeched.

Lady Ashley looked at the people who had gathered around. "Is there anyone else here who has not tried on the ring?"

Isaac pushed Elton forward. "He hasn't, my lady."

When Elton approached her, Lady Ashley took his hand in hers. His hand was callused and tan, except for the white band around his finger where the missing ring had once been.

Lady Ashley slid the ring on Elton's finger with ease. It fit perfectly. "Why did you run away?" she asked.

"You are a lady," answered Elton. "Although I was born a nobleman, since my father's death I've been living the life of a mere stable hand."

"Your character, not your rank, is what captured my

heart," said Lady Ashley with a smile.

Elton looked at all the people, then turned back to Lady Ashley and said, "When my stepmother banished me to the stables, I was too young to fight back. Now I want what is rightfully mine so I can go to your father and ask for your hand in marriage." Then he smiled, pulled a black silk scarf out of his pocket, and added, "By the way, I have been meaning to return this to you." They both laughed as Elton draped the scarf around Lady Ashley's neck.

And so the two were married. News of the marriage traveled quickly throughout the land, as did word of how Elton's stepmother and Miles had mistreated him all those years. The two decided to leave the country and were not heard from again.

Isaac, Elton's dear friend, was not forgotten. If not for him, Elton and Lady Ashley probably never would have met again. To show his gratitude, Elton promoted Isaac to head stable master. When the weather was fine, Isaac would saddle up two horses, and Elton and Lady Ashley would gallop across the meadows and into the forest, where they'd first met.

Red Riding Hood and the Scrawny Little Wolf

BY MARY QUATTLEBAUM

Lou lived with her daddy in a house tucked into the side of a mountain. She was a bold girl, fond of ranging freely through forest and field. She knew the ways of the wild things and respected bat, hare, and baby bear alike. Folks smiled when she whistled by.

One fine morning, after a big breakfast of porridge and toast, Lou's daddy said, "Lou-girl, I'm fixin' to make my famous five-bean vegetable soup."

"Yum," said Lou, piling bowls in the sink.

"I'll do those dishes," said Daddy. "What I really need right now is a cord of wood. Gotta keep a good blaze going under this pot." He tapped the black pot with his huge spoon.

Lou picked up her ax. "Do you want me to stop by Granny's?" she asked.

"Nah. At this time of day she's probably out leaping tree stumps for exercise," said Daddy, "or playing tug-of-war with her mule. You won't catch her at home."

"I'll bring her a bucket of soup for supper," said Lou, swinging out the door.

"Oh, she's coming over, by and by," hollered Daddy. "Now fetch me that wood quick, please. This measly fire won't burn for long."

So off went Lou, with her fine ax on her shoulder and a whistle on her lips. The wildflowers sparkled like tiny suns, and a breeze frisked through the mountain grass. The puffy clouds seemed close enough to touch. It was a lovely morning indeed.

That's why Lou was shocked when she rounded a bend in the path and found a girl crying as if her heart were breaking.

"Hey," said Lou, stopping short. "What's with the tears?"

"I am Little Red Riding Hood," wept the child, "and I am a heroine."

"You don't say?" Lou was impressed. She knew about heroines from books, of course. A heroine seemed like a grand thing to be, not a reason to cry. "There, there," Lou said. "Tell me your story."

"Well," the girl sniffed, "my grandmother is sick—"

"I'm sorry to hear that," Lou interrupted. "What ails her?"

The girl blew her nose into a lace hanky. "I don't know." She sniffed again. "It's not important. Anyway, I'm bringing her this basket of goodies—"

"When my granny is sick, she drinks lots of orange juice and eats plenty of soup," Lou said. "Liquids are important when you're fighting a cold."

"Well, *my* grandmother likes goodies," said Red Riding Hood. "Which brings me back to my story—"

"Goodies!" Lou took a pretty little cake from the pretty little basket and inspected it. "This food is no good for a sick person. You can't build up a body with cakes."

"In *my* story you can." The girl glared. "Now, if I may please continue—"

"Cakes!" Lou shook her head. "My daddy makes a five-bean soup that could heal a bull with one hoof in the grave."

"I WAS ON THE PATH TO MY POOR SICK GRANDMOTHER'S," yelled the girl, "when I was DETAINED by a WOLF—"

"A wolf?" Lou stopped shaking her head over the little cakes and peered at the girl with interest. "Wolves are quite rare these days. I've never seen one."

"Well, there's one," the girl snapped, pointing. "The lazy thing. He's supposed to eat my grandmother and then try to eat me. But he absolutely refuses. He has ruined my story."

For the first time, Lou noticed a scrawny wolf sitting nearby. "Pleased to make your acquaintance," she said.

"Charmed," said the wolf, nodding politely. "Please explain to this silly girl that I have absolutely no interest in consuming her sick grandmother, her skinny self, or that ridiculous basket of cakes." The wolf shuddered. "I won't eat just anything, you know. I have my pride."

"But it's in the *story!*" Red Riding Hood stomped her foot.

"Well," yawned the wolf, "I want a revision."

"But that's impossible," wailed Red Riding Hood. "The woodsman comes and chops you up. And I live happily ever after."

"But *I* don't," the wolf pointed out.

Lou had to admit the wolf had a point. She thought over Red Riding Hood's tale. There was another problem, too. "No woodsmen in these parts," she said, "unless you count me."

"A woods*woman?*" sniffed Red Riding Hood. "I don't think so."

"Now, Ms. Lou," coaxed the wolf, "there's no reason to chop me up."

"Can't see that there is," agreed Lou.

"What about my story?" Red Riding Hood cried.

"Your story has grown boring," said the wolf. He curled up and tucked his nose under his bushy tail. "Time for a nap."

"WAKE UP!" screamed Red Riding Hood. "Try to eat me."

"Zzzzz," snored the wolf.

"Woodswoman," the girl yelled at Lou. "Do something."

"Hold on now, Little Red Riding Hood." Lou took a deep breath. "Whew! That is one mouthful of a name. Do you mind if I call you Red?"

"Yes, I do! You must use my entire name."

"It just seems so long-like and unfriendly." Lou

shook her head.

"You're certainly not a woodsman." The girl surveyed Lou from head to toe. "But you'll have to do. Now wake up that wolf, and let's get on with my story."

"Oh, little sister," Lou said, continuing to shake her head, "you are one grouchy girl. I don't cotton to commands. Didn't your mama teach you manners?"

"I don't have to say 'please.'" Red Riding Hood was red with rage. "I'm the heroine. This is *my* story."

"Well, I'm with the wolf, then." Lou shouldered her ax. "This story *has* grown mighty boring. I'll be on my way, Little Red. My daddy taught me to leave any situation that gets me riled, and he also taught me to speak out against injustice. I would advise you to be nicer to the next woodswoman who comes along. And leave that poor wolf alone. There's no need to chop up a creature just to suit your story."

"But—but—" sputtered Red Riding Hood.

"Good day." Lou tipped her hat before walking away. Red Riding Hood threw a queen-sized fit! The mountain had never witnessed such stomping and screeching. The wildflowers shivered, the puffy clouds scattered, and the birds were scared silent. But the wolf slept on.

Lou cut her cord of wood and headed on home.

Daddy built up the fire under the soup pot, and they both settled down to wait for their meal.

"Learn anything new while you were out?" Daddy asked.

"I heard a story," said Lou, "about a girl named Little Red Riding Hood."

"Ah, yes." Daddy nodded. "A very old tale."

"Well," Lou said, "I think it's being revised." She then told Daddy all about her encounter with the little girl and the wolf.

Daddy listened with interest and shook his head along with Lou at the girl's foolishness. Finally, he gave the bubbling soup a stir and reached for some bowls. "Well, daughter," he said, dishing it up, "dig in!"

Lou grabbed her spoon and took a steaming bite. "Delicious," she said. "I think this is your best batch yet."

Daddy bowed, then set his own bowl on the table.

Just then they heard a knock at the door. "Must be Granny," said Daddy, opening it. And there she stood, as hale as the heavens were high, with the scrawny wolf beside her.

Granny thumped the mud from her boots, then delivered hugs all around. "I invited a friend," she told Daddy and Lou. "A new friend close to starvin'. Do you mind?"

"Come in! Sit down!" Daddy threw the door wide. "Let me get some bowls."

The poor wolf was so hungry, he drooled as Daddy set a steaming bowl of soup before him. He dabbed at his mouth with a napkin, then sniffed deeply. "It smells superb. My compliments to the chef."

Daddy beamed as the wolf slurped up the soup. He heaped the wolf's bowl again and again. Finally, the creature leaned back and sighed contentedly.

"It does my heart good to see such a healthy appetite," said Daddy.

"How's Little Red Riding Hood?" Lou asked the wolf.

"She went on to her grandmother's house without me." The wolf wiped his whiskers. "She's determined to make her tale work."

"That child!" Granny snorted. "She insists on bringing nothing but cakes to my poor friend Miranda. No one can get well on a diet of sugar. Miranda just gets sicker and sicker."

"Let's bring her some soup!" Daddy hollered, spooning some into his biggest crock.

"Don't forget orange juice," said Granny. "We should bring a big jug of it."

"Red Riding Hood won't be happy about this," warned the wolf. "She has her heart set on goodies and a vicious wolf."

"Not to mention a woodsman," said Lou.

Lou, Daddy, Granny, and the wolf decided that Miranda's health was more important than her granddaughter's misguided story. They set off down the mountain path with their soup and juice. Soon they arrived at Miranda's cottage and knocked on the door. Miranda was delighted to see them. In fact, she downed her soup as quick as a starving wolf and soon started feeling much better. They all had just settled down for a cozy chat when there was a loud *rat-tat-tat* on the door.

"Grandmother," Little Red Riding Hood called. "I know you're in there."

"That child!" Miranda said, diving under the covers. "She'll be the death of me."

The door flew open and Red Riding Hood stomped in. "That stupid wolf has disap . . ." She saw the wolf and brightened.

"I trust you're well," the wolf said politely.

"Ha!" shouted Red Riding Hood. "I *knew* you'd be back, you big bad wolf. You were about to eat my grandmother, weren't you?"

"Please," Miranda begged, "not today."

"Certainly not, dear," the wolf soothed Miranda. To Red Riding Hood, he added, "Do hang up your hood and join us. May I offer you some soup?"

"It's quite nice," peeped Miranda.

"Grandmother!" Red Riding Hood exploded. "You're supposed to eat my goodies."

"But they're stale!" wailed Miranda.

"Hold on, now, Little Red." Lou stepped into the fray. "We came to pay a friendly call on your granny, and you seem bent on ruining it."

"But my story—"

"Has been revised," finished Lou. "Now take that bowl and thank the kind wolf."

But Red Riding Hood would have none of the five-bean soup and, in a rage, she ate the entire basket of hard-as-rock goodies. She went home with a chipped tooth and a stomachache.

"And so the heroine departs," murmured Lou as the group watched Red Riding Hood stomp down the path.

The wolf put on the kettle for tea and smiled at Miranda, Granny, Daddy, and Lou. "Now *this* is my idea of happily ever after," he said.

Hansel and Gretel

BY TIMOTHY TOCHER

Weekends are strange. You just can't predict how they're going to turn out. My name is Hansel, and if you've got a few minutes, I'll tell you about the bizarre weekend I just had.

Friday started off fine. I got home from school, collected my weekly allowance, and hopped a bus to the mall. Man, it felt great to have a pocketful of money and lots of free time.

Some days I'm desperate enough to eat in the school cafeteria. But on Fridays I know my allowance is coming, so I skip lunch to enjoy the mall cuisine. I circled the food court and ate from half a dozen stands: burgers, tacos, pizza, ice cream, popcorn, and about a gallon of soda to wash it all down.

Then I hit the baseball card store and bought a bunch of rookie cards. I'd never heard of any of these guys, but if they make it big, the cards will be worth a fortune! My next stop was the arcade. Before I knew it, I had only one quarter left.

How can a guy live on such a skimpy allowance? And why do my parents waste their money by giving it to my sister, Gretel? All she does is hoard hers. As soon as she gets it, she shoves the money in her piggybank.

Without enough for bus fare, I faced a long walk home. I figured I might as well be completely broke, so I stopped at the candy store near the mall entrance. Maybe I could buy something for a quarter.

I didn't even bother looking on the top shelves, where the expensive, popular brands are displayed. I bent down to check the dusty boxes on the bottom shelf. They all looked pretty nasty. I was about to give up when I spotted a label I'd never seen before: "Old Witch Licorice Nose Warts 25¢—You can't go wrong when you pick the Old Witch's nose!" Who could resist? I handed over my last quarter and started home.

I plucked a Nose Wart from the box and popped it in my mouth. I didn't expect much from such a cheap candy, but it was great! The warts were really sweet and so chewy, they lasted all the way home. Even after dinner, I could still taste Nose Warts—some had stuck in between my teeth.

I locked the door to my room to keep my nosy sister out and flopped down on my bed. There was one Nose Wart left and I sucked it to make it last. As I studied the package, I noticed some writing on the back: "Visit our factory outlet. Buy direct from the Old Witch and save!" There was even a little map. The outlet was part of a mall that had just opened a few miles from town. If I had money, I thought, I'd shoot out there and stock up on Nose Warts.

I must have fallen asleep shortly after that, because when I woke up it was morning. Cool, I was already dressed! I couldn't get that candy off my mind, so I decided to lower myself and ask Gretel for a loan.

I crossed the hall and tapped politely on her door. There was no answer. "Gretel, it's me," I said. She still didn't answer, so I tried the doorknob. It was unlocked!

I slipped into her sorry excuse for a room. A grownup might as well live in there! All her clothes were on hangers and her bed was made. Her stuffed animals were lined up on shelves, each in its place. Even her desk was neat. Her Nancy Drew books were stacked on one side, and her enormous piggy bank anchored the other.

When I saw the pig, I did a double take. It was so jammed with money that dollar bills were sticking out of the slot in its back. I crossed the room and picked it up, just to see how heavy it was. Wow! I was surprised her desk could hold that much weight.

Now, ordinarily, I'm a pretty honest guy, but I couldn't bear the thought of all that money sitting there while I wasted a Saturday doing nothing. I looked up and down the hall to make sure no one was coming and ducked back into my room. I snatched my backpack off the floor and dumped out my school books. Then I snuck back into Gretel's room.

First I used a key to pry the bills out of the slot. Then I shook out the coins and dumped them into my backpack. When I had filled the pack halfway, I stuck the dollar bills back where they had been. Unless you picked up the pig, there was no way to tell anything was missing.

I swung the heavy pack over my shoulders and headed for the bus stop. I was back in action!

When I got off the bus, I saw that the outlet mall was designed to look like an old-time village. I checked out the directory, but there was no listing for the Old

Witch. Before I could panic, I noticed a sweet licorice smell. My nose would lead me to that Old Witch better than any directory could.

I followed my nose past shoe stores, toy stores, and clothing stores. Lots of grownups were sitting in the plaza sipping weird coffee drinks. I walked on and on, lugging my backpack full of coins, as the licorice smell grew stronger.

Finally I came to the last store and stood facing a fence that separated the mall from a run-down house. My mouth was watering from the strong smell of Nose Warts, but where the heck were they?

Then I noticed a piece of cardboard hanging from the fence. Sloppy magic marker letters spelled out "Old Witch Outlet." An arrow pointed to a gap in the fence. I walked through the gap and across a patch of weeds toward the old house. What a weird setup. My eyes told me this couldn't be the place, but my schnoz insisted, "Oh yes it is!"

The front door was locked, but another sign directed me to a side screen door. I went in and sure enough: Nose Wart Central. Boxes of Nose Warts were stacked from floor to ceiling. I headed straight for the economy-size boxes to check the price. What a deal!

The place seemed deserted. I went over to the counter and emptied my backpack. I began sorting the mountain of change into stacks of nickels, dimes, and quarters so I could figure out how much I had. The pack didn't seem nearly as full as it had been at home, but maybe it was my imagination. I stuffed enough money for bus fare into my pocket. No way was I walking all the way home from here!

I was trying to figure out how many dollars forty-six quarters made when a voice right behind me screeched, "It looks like you robbed a piggy bank, sonny!"

I jumped so high that I sent my whole stack of quarters flying. As I scrambled to gather them up from the floor, I peered up at the person who had startled me. She wore scuffed combat boots; a long, baggy, black skirt; and a purple blouse with puffy sleeves. Her wrinkled face was framed by a mane of thick gray hair—enough to cover every bald head in an old-folks home. But what really caught my attention was the huge, pickle-shaped wart which grew from the end of her nose. This had to be the Old Witch!

"Did I scare you, sonny?" she cackled. "I often have that effect on people, but I'm quite harmless. Are you here to buy some Nose Warts?"

I tried not to stare at her wart, but it was like trying not to look at a scary scene in a movie—you keep peeking whether you want to or not. When I found my voice, I bought all the Nose Warts I could afford. As I loaded my backpack, the Old Witch surprised me again.

"Stay here and watch the place, and I'll give you six more boxes," she said. "I have to run an important errand."

Before I could argue, she swept all the coins into a sack and scooted out the back door. A few seconds later she roared past on a beat-up old Harley with a sidecar.

It was kind of cool being in charge of the store. I was sure I could handle any customers who showed up. All the prices were marked, and there was an old-fashioned cash register where you just bang some keys and the drawer opens. I figured it would be good advertising to show I liked the product, so I helped myself to a new box of Nose Warts and popped a few in my mouth.

A half-hour went by, and the sugar from the Nose Warts had me ready to bounce off the walls. Suddenly, the screen door jerked open. There stood a sight scarier than any old witch. It was Gretel!

"Where's my money, you thief?" she howled.

All I could think to say was, "How'd you find me?"

Pretty lame, huh?

"Do you think I read all those Nancy Drew books for nothing?" she asked. "I followed the clues. A trail of coins led all the way to the bus stop. And you left a candy box with a map lying on my desk. If you spent my money on candy, you're in big trouble!"

"Not just candy, Gretel—Nose Warts. I bought some for you, too. You're going to love them."

"Get a refund right now!" demanded Gretel.

I heard the Harley roar past again. I peeked out the screen door and saw that the sidecar was loaded with bags. "She's got your money, Gretel. Go talk to her." I pointed toward the door, and Gretel hurried out.

I picked up my backpack and sure enough: there was a tear in one corner just big enough for coins to slide through. What rotten luck! I didn't know whether to run for it or wait and see what the Old Witch said to Gretel. Finally my curiosity won out. I stepped outside. Gretel had her hands on her hips and looked pretty mad.

"The money's gone, dear," said the Old Witch. "How was I to know it wasn't his?"

"Well, open the cash register and pay me from there," demanded Gretel.

The Old Witch sighed. "There's nothing in that

register. I spent every penny on licorice root, corn syrup, and sugar. I have to make lots of Nose Warts if I want 'em to catch on."

"How do you expect to sell candy in this dump?" asked Gretel, waving her arm at the old house. "Most people aren't like my brother. They want to buy candy from a clean, modern store."

"I know, but I can't pay the rent on a new store until people start buying my candy," explained the Old Witch. "If I could sell every box of Nose Warts in this house, I'd have enough money to lease a store on the other side of the fence."

My sister put her hands behind her back, stared at the ground, and began pacing. The Old Witch looked at me, puzzled.

"Don't worry," I said, "Gretel does this when she's thinking. It works for Nancy Drew, so she thinks it'll help her."

Watching Gretel pace was like watching a Ping-Pong game in slow motion. Just as my eyes were starting to glaze over, she shrieked.

"I've got it! Hansel can walk around the outlet plaza giving free samples from his backpack, along with a map to help people find your store. When your candy sells out, you can pay me back."

The Old Witch's eyes sparkled. "What a great idea! When people try my candy, I know they'll like it!" Then her face fell. "But is your brother willing to do it?"

I was about to ask "What's in it for me?" when Gretel went postal.

"Is he willing?" she shouted. "How about it, Hansel? You can either give out free samples for a few days or explain to Mom and Dad how you stole money from my piggy bank. Your choice."

Some choice. For the rest of the weekend I trudged around that hokey mall, trying to give away candy. It's not as easy as it sounds. You should see the looks people gave me when I asked if they'd like some Nose Warts. My feet are killing me from all the walking. One thing I swear: even if I live long enough to grow my own nose wart, I'll never go in Gretel's room again.

We have to wait until next Saturday to see if the Old Witch can pay back Gretel's money. If not, I'm still the boy with the free samples. I have a feeling it's going to be another long, hard weekend for yours truly.

But, hey, you never know. Weekends are strange!

Katie and the Dragon

BY RISA HUTSON

"He's done it again!" gasped Princess Violet, bursting into her sister Katie's room and feigning a faint on the bed.

Katie rolled her eyes. Violet was always so dramatic. "Who's done what?" she asked.

"Father has offered one of us in marriage as a reward to any prince who can defeat that awful green dragon," said Violet, sitting up on the bed.

"Don't tell me that obnoxious dragon is back?" Katie shook her head in disbelief. "Just six months ago, Prince Andrew defeated the dragon and married Lila.

I'm just glad he didn't pick me."

"Father doesn't seem to realize how risky this 'beat the dragon and choose your bride' game is," said Violet. "One of us is sure to be chosen by someone horrible. If only we had secret loves who could defeat the dragon."

Katie blushed and looked away quickly.

Violet noticed. "Surely *you* don't have a secret love!"

"Well, what if I do?" said Katie.

"Who on earth is it?"

"Someone I can live happily ever after with—certainly not some vain, boring old prince," said Katie firmly. "I want to marry someone who makes me laugh . . . like Colin."

"Colin? You mean the court jester?! You must be joking!" exclaimed Violet.

Just then a maid burst into the room. "I'm sorry to interrupt, Your Highnesses," she said, "but I knew you'd want to hear this right away: Prince Wadsworth is traveling here to fight the dragon!" The maid then quickly looked down the hall and left the room.

"Oh, great," grumbled Katie. "Prince Worthless is more like it."

"Prince Wadsworth is horrible," said Violet. "What

if he wins?"

"Remember the last time he visited? All he did was eat, hunt, and admire himself in the mirror. He is one of the stupidest, vainest princes ever," said Katie.

"Of course, he's always so polite in front of Father," said Violet. "Father thinks he's wonderful."

"We can't just wait and see what happens. We have to do something," said Katie. "Let's go visit the dragon."

"Oh no! Dragons are dangerous!" Violet protested. "That dragon could roast us crispy with a single breath!"

"Well, which is worse: facing a dragon or marrying Prince Worthless?"

"*Anything* would be better than marrying *him*," admitted Violet.

And so it was settled. The princesses quickly donned their hiking boots and went off in search of the dragon. They found him sleeping in a sunny field.

Violet stopped at the edge of the field and said, "Katie, you're so clever. I think you should be the one to talk to the dragon."

"Well, all right," said Katie reluctantly. "I'll see what I can do."

As Violet huddled near the trees, Katie took a deep breath and walked toward the dragon's huge head.

"Excuse me, Mr. Dragon," called Katie, trying to sound brave.

The dragon snorted awake. He peered at Katie with his large green eyes. Katie curtsied, and the dragon nodded politely.

"Handsome dragon, please tell me why you have returned," said Katie.

The dragon smiled and said, "You must be the next reward for whoever gets me to leave your kingdom."

"The winner can choose either me or my sister." She gestured towards Violet.

"Why is she waiting over there?" asked the dragon.

"She's not used to speaking with dragons. She just wanted to admire you from afar. You are a most extraordinary dragon," said Katie. She'd heard that dragons were very vain and loved compliments.

"I can tell that *you* know how to speak to a dragon," he said, straightening up a bit to show off his glistening scales.

"It's an honor and a pleasure to speak with you, Sir. But please tell me . . . why do you keep returning to our kingdom?"

"You are very brave to confront me. For that you deserve an honest answer." The dragon paused and blew a few smoke rings. Then he said, "Your father pays me very well."

"Father arranged this?!" exclaimed Katie.

"Of course. He wants to make sure you marry well, so I agreed to let the prince of his choice chase me away. I certainly don't want to get hurt, and believe me, neither does any so-called brave knight. Many kings with daughters make such arrangements. Sometimes we even rehearse a performance if a prince wants to appear especially daring."

The dragon went on. "This way the prince wins the princess with no risk of being rejected. The king feels he has arranged the best possible marriage for his daughter. Both the king and the prince pay me, so I come out very well indeed. The only one who might not be happy about all this is . . . well . . . the princess."

Katie was shocked by the dragon's revelations, but she suspected that they were true. Her father was still gloating over how well Lila's marriage turned out. But the practice certainly wasn't fair to princesses who didn't love the knights who won them. Suddenly she remembered the problem at hand. "Have you made a deal with Prince Wadsworth?" she asked.

"As a matter of fact, I have, but I don't like him very

much. I pity whichever of you he chooses. He's such a coward. He made me promise he wouldn't get hurt, then whined about my fee. He only wants to marry one of you because your father is so wealthy."

"Unfortunately, neither I nor my sister want to marry him. Is there any way we could persuade you to help us?" she asked.

"I doubt you could top your father's payment," said the dragon.

"What is he paying you?" asked Katie.

"Two treasure chests recovered from a sunken pirate ship," answered the dragon.

Katie frowned. There was no way she and Violet could beat that. She'd heard dragons loved treasure more than anything. Her brows knit as she tried to think of another plan.

The dragon couldn't help liking Katie and didn't want to see her looking so troubled. "I wish I could help you," he said. "Whom would you like to marry?"

"I would much rather marry Colin, the court jester," said Katie. "He is brave, kind, and very funny."

The dragon grinned. He definitely liked this down-to-earth princess.

Katie thought a bit longer. "Several knights will

challenge you tomorrow," she said. "How will you tell one from another if they're all wearing armor?"

"The princes who pay me always wear orange scarves on their helmets," said the dragon.

Katie smiled and bowed to the dragon. "Thank you, kind dragon, for that information. Remember: Father will still pay you if you make an 'honest' mistake."

The dragon watched Katie walk away and join her sister. He pondered her comment and decided that if there were any way to help her and still get the treasure, he would try it.

The next morning, seven knights came to battle the dragon. The king, the princesses, and villagers watched from a nearby hill. The dragon quickly knocked two knights off their horses with a swipe of his tail. A blast of fiery breath sent two more galloping away. Another knight dropped his reins and sat wide-eyed in terror as his horse wandered off to nibble on a clump of grass.

Two knights remained, and from each one's helmet, a bright orange scarf flapped in the wind. The dragon turned questioningly toward the king. The king just shrugged. He didn't know which knight was Wadsworth, either.

Both knights bowed to the princesses. Then one

knight poked the other's horse with his lance, making the horse rear up. The second knight somersaulted off the horse and landed on his feet. He bowed to the cheering crowd, then remounted his horse while twirling his lance. The lance smacked the first knight, knocking him into a puddle. After slipping and falling a few times (much to the crowd's entertainment), the muddy knight managed to remount his horse.

The dragon, who'd been trying hard not to laugh, took a deep breath and roared so loud, the ground shook. The muddy knight covered his ears and quaked with fear. The other knight bravely charged and thrust his lance strong and straight. It pierced the dragon's shoulder, making him bellow and fly away. The villagers cheered wildly.

The muddy knight recovered his wits and galloped ahead of the other knight toward the king. He dismounted, took off his helmet, and flung it on the ground. He was Prince Wadsworth. "It's not fair!" he whined. "I should have won."

The king said, "I'm sorry, Wadsworth, but your opponent chased off the dragon. I can't go back on my word. He may choose one of my daughters." Wadsworth stomped off in a huff.

The crowd cheered as the victor came forward. The princesses waited anxiously to see who he was. He bowed to the king and removed his helmet. The villagers gasped and murmured among themselves.

"Why, you're not a prince. You're not even a nobleman. You . . . you're my court jester!" stammered the king. "This is ridiculous. I can't let one of my daughters marry you!"

"Father," said Katie, "Colin has won fairly."

The king turned red with anger and humiliation. "Go ahead and choose," he finally choked out.

"I choose Princess Katie," said Colin. Katie stepped forward and took his hand. Her heart thumped as she gazed into his kind blue eyes. He untied the orange scarf from his helmet, handed it to her, and whispered, "I believe this belongs to you."

Katie winked at Colin and he winked back. Then, looking as serious as she could, she faced her father. "Father, if Violet picks her own husband, do you think she could do worse than a jester?"

"I guess not," he said grudgingly. "Violet may choose her own husband. Just don't come complaining to me if you choose badly." He glanced at Colin and said to Katie, "Katie, I hope you won't blame me for this disaster."

"I would have blamed you if Wadsworth had won. But instead I'll thank you for arranging a very happy marriage," said Katie. The king sighed, shook his head, and walked away.

Katie squeezed Colin's hand and turned toward Violet. "I told you I planned to live happily ever after."

Violet smiled and said, "Thanks to you, I'll be able to live happily ever after, too."

Far away, in his cave, the dragon pulled the lance from his tough scales. It hurt no worse than a sliver. With one roar he'd been able to tell which knight was the cowardly Wadsworth and which was the brave jester. As he sorted through his pirate treasure, the dragon chuckled. He liked Katie, and it had cost him nothing to help her.

Author Biographies

Risa Hutson currently lives in Sandy, Utah, but will always consider herself an Oregonian. She has three boys and a girl who keep her very busy. Growing up, Risa loved reading books—fairy tales and fantasy were her favorites. "Katie and the Dragon" is her first published story. She is now working on a young adult novel and several short stories.

Bruce Lansky, the author of "The Girl Who Wanted to Be a Princess," has been writing stories about clever, courageous girls for *Girls to the Rescue*, a series he also edits. Bruce also enjoys writing funny poetry, some of which can be found in *Poetry Party*, and performing in school assemblies and teacher conferences. He has two grown children and currently lives with his computer near a beautiful lake in Minnesota.

Jude Mandell, the author of "A Thoroughly Modern Rapunzel," is a writer for *The Wedding Pages Bride and Home Magazine* and teaches writing and communication skills at National-Louis University in Chicago. She is the author of a mystery-adventure book, *Buffalo Blinkie and the Crazy Circus Caper*, and in 1989 won the Golden Heart Award from the Romance Writers of America for an adult historical novel. In addition, she has designed a phonics program that is in use throughout the country.

Liya Lev Oertel wrote "The Fairy Godfather" because she felt that not only should women be able to do "men's work," but men should be equally allowed to do "women's work"—and the fairy profession is one of the last to be cracked. Liya is originally from Minsk, Byelorussia, and has lived in the United States for eighteen years. Liya graduated from Brown University and currently works as an editor and lives in Minneapolis, Minnesota, with her husband, Jens. Liya has published stories in *Girls to the Rescue, Book #4*, and in *Newfangled Fairy Tales, Book #1*.

Mary Quattlebaum wrote "Red Riding Hood and the Scrawny Little Wolf" because she felt the wolf got a bad rap in the original story. Mary is the author of seven award-winning children's books, including *Jackson Jones* *and the Puddle of Thorns* and *A Year on My Street* (poems), and of many stories and poems in children's magazines, such as *Cricket, Spider, Ladybug,* and *Boys' Life.* She writes frequently for the *Washington Post* and holds a B.A. from the College of William and Mary and an M.A. from Georgetown University. She lives in Washington, D.C., where she and her husband are expecting their first child.

Jason Sanford, the author of "Rumpelstiltskin, Private Eye," has worked as a Peace Corps Volunteer in Thailand, a newspaper reporter in Tuskegee, Alabama, and an archeologist for Auburn University. He currently lives in Minneapolis with his wife, Jennifer, who is a graduate student at the University of Minnesota. Jason was selected as a participant in the 1997–98 Loft Mentor Series for Fiction and has a story in *Girls to the Rescue, Book #4.*

Rita Schlachter, the author of "The Gold Ring," lives in Cincinnati, Ohio, with her husband, Phil. She has one son in college, Steven, and two married daughters, Traci and Michelle. Rita has written five books and several magazine stories for children, and has a story in *Newfangled Fairy Tales, Book #1.* In addition to reading and writing, Rita enjoys helping her daughter Traci—who works with the rescue and rehabilitation of wildlife—care for injured and orphaned baby animals.

Timothy Tocher, the author of "The Little Tailor" and "Hansel and Gretel," teaches at George Grant Mason Elementary in Tuxedo, New York. He lives with his wife, Judy, in nearby Rockland County. His humorous poems have been published in *Kids Pick the Funniest Poems, No More Homework! No More Tests!,* and in various magazines for teachers. He also has three stories published in *Newfangled Fairy Tales, Book #1.*

Debra Tracy, the author of "The Clever Princess Who Slept on a Pea," is a home-schooling mom who lives in Farmington, Minnesota, with her husband and four children. She graduated from the University of California at Davis with a degree in English and an emphasis in creative writing. She has published a story in *Spider* and two stories in *Girls to the Rescue, Book #5.* When not writing or teaching, Debra directs a drama ministry at her church, enjoys life in the country, race-walking, hiking, reading, and time spent with her family and friends.

Newfangled Fairy Tales, Book #1

Edited by Bruce Lansky

This is a collection of 10 delightful fairy tales with new twists on old stories and themes, including a modern King Midas who doesn't have time for his son's Little League games and a clever princess who pays a dragon to lose a fight with a prince so she can marry the man she loves.

Order # 2500 **$3.95**

Girls to the Rescue series

Edited by Bruce Lansky

Each anthology in this critically acclaimed series contains folk- and fairy tales featuring clever, courageous, and determined girls from around the world. When girls see this collection, they will say, "Finally! We get to be the heroes." This groundbreaking series updates traditional fairy tales for girls 7–13.

Book #1 Order #2215
Book #2 Order #2216
Book #3 Order #2219
Book #4 Order #2221
Book #5 Order #2222
$3.95 each

Young Marian's Adventures in Sherwood Forest

by Stephen Mooser

In the tradition of *Girls to the Rescue,* this novel-length story tells the exciting tale of 13-year-old Maid Marian, who must battle the evil Sheriff of Nottingham to save her father's life.

Order # 2218 **$4.50**

Order Form

Qty.	Title	Author	Order No.	Unit Cost (U.S. $)	Total
	Bad Case of the Giggles	Lansky, B.	2411	$16.00	
	Free Stuff for Kids	Free Stuff Editors	2190	$5.00	
	Girls to the Rescue, Book #1	Lansky, B.	2215	$3.95	
	Girls to the Rescue, Book #2	Lansky, B.	2216	$3.95	
	Girls to the Rescue, Book #3	Lansky, B.	2219	$3.95	
	Girls to the Rescue, Book #4	Lansky, B.	2221	$3.95	
	Girls to the Rescue, Book #5	Lansky, B.	2222	$3.95	
	Happy Birthday to Me!	Lansky, B.	2416	$8.95	
	Just for Fun Party Game Book	Warner, P.	6065	$3.95	
	Kids Are Cookin'	Brown, K.	2440	$8.00	
	Kids Pick-A-Party Book	Warner, P.	6090	$9.00	
	Kids Pick the Funniest Poems	Lansky, B.	2410	$16.00	
	Kids' Holiday Fun	Warner, P.	6000	$12.00	
	Kids' Party Cookbook	Warner, P.	2435	$12.00	
	Kids' Party Games and Activities	Warner, P.	6095	$12.00	
	Newfangled Fairy Tales, Book #1	Lansky, B.	2500	$3.95	
	Newfangled Fairy Tales, Book #2	Lansky, B.	2501	$3.95	
	No More Homework! No More Tests!	Lansky, B.	2414	$8.00	
	Poetry Party	Lansky, B.	2430	$12.00	
	Young Marian's Adventures	Mooser, S.	2218	$4.50	
				Subtotal	
		Shipping and Handling, see below			
		MN residents add 6.5% sales tax			
				Total	

YES, please send me the books indicated above. Add $2.00 shipping and handling for the first book and $.50 for each additional book. Add $2.50 to total for books shipped to Canada. Overseas postage will be billed. Allow up to four weeks for delivery. Send check or money order payable to Meadowbrook Press. No cash or C.O.D.'s please. Prices subject to change without notice. **Quantity discounts available upon request.**

Send book(s) to:

Name_____

Address _____

City _____State _____ Zip _____

Telephone (_____) _____

Purchase order number (if necessary) _____

Payment via:

☐ Check or money order payable to Meadowbrook (No cash or C.O.D.'s please)
    Amount enclosed $_____

☐ Visa (for orders over $10.00 only)   ☐ MasterCard (for orders over $10.00 only)

Account # _____

Signature _____ Exp. Date_____

You can also phone us for orders of $10.00 or more at 1-800-338-2232.

A *FREE* Meadowbrook catalog is available upon request.

Mail to: Meadowbrook Press, 5451 Smetana Drive, Minnetonka, MN 55343
Phone (612) 930-1100   Toll-Free 1-800-338-2232   Fax (612) 930-1940